GLASS HOUSE

LOUIS ARMAND

EQUUS

ISBN 978-0-9931955-7-0

Equus Press
Birkbeck College (William Rowe), 43 Gordon Square, London,
WC1 H0PD, United Kingdom

Cover, typeset and design: lazarus
Composed in 10pt Caslon, composed by William Caslon in 1734.

An excerpt comprising the first two "Qwertz" chapters previously appeared in
Minor Literature[s] magazine.

GLASS
HOUSE

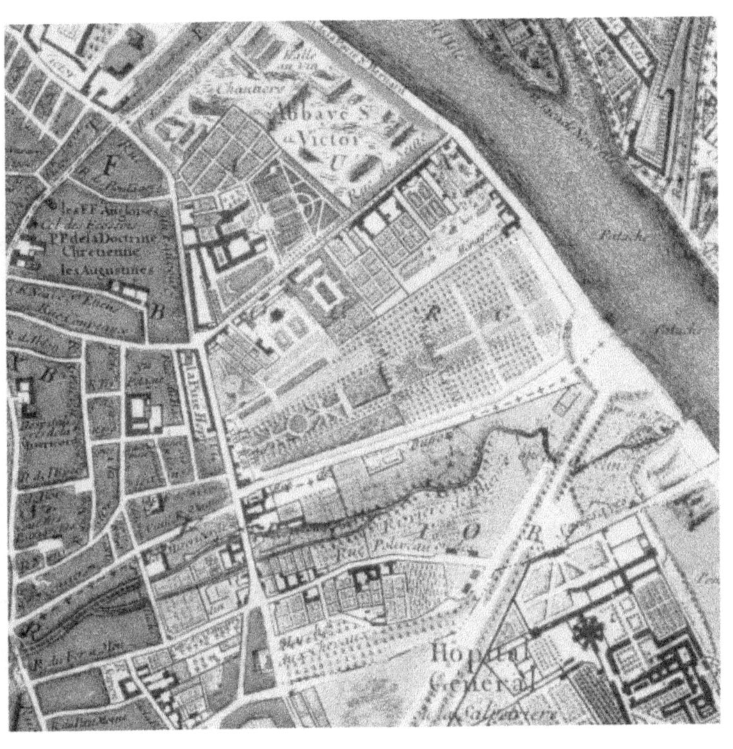

Plan du Jardin des Plantes, Paris, 1794
(Muséum National d'Histoire Naturelles)

À ces mots, il s'est tu.

Assez de mots! Il c'est tué.

Part I

Yadlun

By turns gnarled, tuberous, the mythic upturned baobab enfolded the sky: a hundred-thousand blinking insect monitors up there among the roots & branches trellising through predawn down to their Earth-bound watcher, Yadlun, perched myopic-eyed atop a rusty tennis umpire's chair in the excavated yaw of what once was the courtyard – *Délégation à l'Outre-Mer, Direction des Collections* – of the National Botanical Institute, Jardin des Plantes, 5ème Arrondissement, Paris, France, Europe, Earth, Orion-Cygnus Arm of the Milky Way, Local Interstellar Cloud, C.O.D. He sat there like a firstlast weed among the wastes.

With a melancholic's sense of all-that-impends, Yadlun's gaze rested upon the vista of redbrick emerging, by shadowy facets, from the boundary of the excavation site. Here & there the tampered evidence of an archway, a walled-up tunnel leading nowhere, flanged buttresses standing out of the soil with all the aplomb of fossilised angiosperms in stages of blight. All of which, until the bulldozers arrived, having lain there, unsuspected, for how long? Yadlun peered into the gloom. Who knew what further revelation awaited beneath the tennis court clay. Roman bunkers? Clovis's baptismal bath? A Cluny outhouse with vellum dunny-paper?

They'd begun dismantling it late on a Wednesday afternoon during the meeting of the Household Committee. Yadlun had observed their progress with characteristic squint: a bobcat levelling the overgrowth beneath which the court itself had for decades been submerged. Men in orange reflective vests & hardhats wielded sledgehammers & powersaws at the termite-riddled bleachers & ivy-entangled chainlink, hewing the posts flush with the ground. Then they proceeded to demolish the clubhouse. It wasn't much, a shack flaked with whitewash tenanted by the Institute's cat colony summarily rendered destitute, stalking the periphery, forlorn. Half-a-dozen of them presently mewled around the foot of the umpire's chair, demanding to be fed. Yadlun blinked down at them, shapeshifting in the twilight.

Soon the peacocks in the animal enclosure would startle awake, hooting through the trees. The fluorescents would come on in the Institute, casting checkerboard shadows across the courtyard. Yadlun would tiredly raise his eyes to his office window & find Madame Lenoir's silhouette there – she who'd been his keeper so long he cared not to remember. Knowing how she'd secretly grown ashamed of him, his queer vigils down in the Hole perched foolish atop that highchair like Stylite over his congregation, caught rabbit-eyed in the crisscross of the lights. At 5:15 sharp she'd come down to distribute her meagre charity among the cats, as she always did, & lead Yadlun, unresisting, back inside.

Schönbrunn

Midnight was already long ago. Schönbrunn had his back to the entrance when Laborde slouched in. The bar was half a block from Place Voltaire, a nameless dump with the plaster rotting off the walls. The owner, a heavy-set blonde, was a native of Bastille, French like Le Pen was French. It was the last joint on the street not yet run by "kikes," "negras" or "gooks." By the next arrondissement, you may as well've been in East Jerusalem already. Laborde took the only other stool at the counter, carefully draping his huge buttocks over the seat. Then, in what seemed a continuous motion, the large man tipped himself back from the bar, pinched his nose & jetted a stream of snot over his right shoulder onto the linoleum.

Schönbrunn, ignoring the intrusion, turned his glass pensively between thumb & index finger, & signalled for a refill. Someone coughed. In the background Johnny Halliday bawled about a hard-luck dame while a guitar faded in & out of the static. Laborde straightened, dragged the back of his hand across his mouth, ogling his companion dully through a pair of wire-rimmed specs that sloped inveterately ten degrees east to west. He stabbed a porcine finger at the notebook lying shut between Schönbrunn's glass & a loose stack of coins. Cop standard. Schönbrunn never used it except to jot down bits of drunken insight he'd sometimes later meditate on sober, when the spirit moved him, but he wasn't there yet.

—What's the word for today?

Laborde spoke in a large voice that turned heads in the small room. His eyes, *two pissholes in the snow*, fixed on a spot where his interlocutor's three-day moustache grazed a flabby upper lip. The largeness of Laborde's talk overcompensated for an inner voice that was cramped, stuttering & as emasculated as the sagging dugs filling out the front of his canary-yellow polyester shirt. An inner voice he'd've secretly been ashamed of were he ever to admit it was his — afraid anyone in the immediate vicinity would be able to tune in on it if he didn't drown it out with the noise his mouth produced. But if Laborde was self-conscious in this respect, it extended to no other part of his visible, audible, or olfactory being.

—Shite, mumbled Schönbrunn, pocketing the notebook.

Laborde, who reminded him of an elephant with a layer of jaundiced ash beneath its hide, rolled around to face the bar. There were large half-moons under his arms. A line of sweat had congealed in the groove of his chin. The collar of his shirt had turned faintly amber.

—Shite with spangles on, Laborde enlarged. Enlarging was his stock-in-trade. Make it two of those, he told the blonde behind the counter, sizing her up.

The blonde poured a couple of Napoléons, the house's finest.

—Voilà, la même punition… she croaked, setting their glasses in front of them, sliding what was left of Schönbrunn's change into her fat paw.

Laborde sniffed at his brandy, brought it to his lips, winced appreciatively, then made a subtle heliotropic movement of his head, pisshole eyes taking in the vista: half-a-dozen regulars hunkered down around plastic tables, minding their drinks, one in the corner on a high stool holding up the wall.

—Just came from Massy. Some kid took a monkey-wrench to her uncle's head while he was asleep. Made a righteous mess of the bastard. Turns out Uncle Ernie used to baby-sit the nieces when they were real young. Got them to take turns sucking him off while he watched the Champion's League replays. No way to verify, of course, without putting them through their paces, *hehe*, but who wants to lie awake at night worrying about where the next monkey-wrench'll come from? We interviewed the other two sisters, but they're next to fracking useless. One says she don't remember, other refuses even to talk. Seems our kid was the tough nut of the family. Didn't try to run or nothing. Just waited till she was sure the sonofabitch was cold, then phoned the switchboard. Left the door unlatched & all. Hardly seems fair, does it?

—Takes all types.

—Sure, Laborde drawled, turning back to his drink. Sure it does.

The brandy disappeared. He smacked his lips.

—Should've seen her. Maybe fourteen, blood all over, still holding the fracking wrench, waiting in front of the telly like she'd just ordered pizza.

Lenoir

The masonic orderliness of Camille Lenoir's daily ritual began in the darkness shy of 4:00a.m. – to the accompaniment of an unbroken stream of sentimental mush that wafted from the wireless on the kitchenette sill & to which the efficiency of her ablutions made stark counterpoint. She was a thin woman, androgynous, not quite a woman: childless, embodying a kind of phylogenetic austerity reminiscent of certain shade-seeking vines. People invariably addressed her as *Madame.* Even in her twenties, it'd always been *Madame* Lenoir, an honorific evoking spinsterial timelessness. Her visage, still, presented to the mirror a virtual doppelganger of that former self. Like very finely cracked bone china. She was, in a quixotic sense, one of those born before her time rather than of it. There was about her a certain air of an epoch forestalled.

The radio prattled. Sacha Distel, *Ça m'ennuie d'aller dîner chez ta mère…*

At a corner of a narrow fold-out counter, a boy sat absorbed in a bowl of lukewarm tea. Madame Lenoir had no idea what the boy's name was, but she called him Gep – for the way, perhaps, he seemed trapped like an insect between window panes. Or perhaps for no reason at all – just to call him something. Anything than simply "boy." *What about the boy? Come here boy? What's your name, boy?* One day he'd simply appeared, trailing Yadlun catlike around the Institute, mute, a second shadow. Yadlun, with his love of stray creatures – the uncharacterisable, belonging to no recognised species, no genus – had taken the boy in.

No-one knew where this Gep had come from, where he belonged. From something approaching charity, Madame Lenoir brought him home. Perhaps, she supposed, a proper meal & a soft place to sleep, for one night, or two at most, might coax something out of the child: a clue, an affection. But Gep hardly even glanced at her, never spoke. She watched him stirring the bowl of tea with his breath – short, long, making something remorseless of it. Or remorseful. It bothered her that she couldn't tell which.

Normally she herself would be sitting where the boy was now sitting, devoting a few moments to a borrowed library book, before driving to the Jardin via the pâtisserie on rue Monge, arriving at the offices of the National Botanical Institute shortly before five o'clock – in time to prepare Yadlun's morning coffee, to feed the cats. *Poor man,* she thought, *going through a rough patch.* The cats, for their part, merely being cats.

The book she was nominally reading lay on the counter beside the radio, a tasselled bookmark sticking out from between the pages. *Massacre at Montségur.* In three weeks she'd managed only one quarter of the Albigensian Crusade. The Army of Christ had just set about the decimation of Béziers on the feast day of Mary Magdalene. *Burnt, too, was the Cathedral that Master Gervais built: so fierce were the flames that it burst asunder, cracked down the midst of it, & collapsed in two halves…*

But this morning, instead of reading, she stood at the sink watching the boy's reflection in the window, washing & rinsing, arranging the few plates on a shelf, the few knives & forks & spoons in a drawer. Her fingers worried themselves. The boy puzzled her. His passive, unresisting silences. She wondered if, after all, he really was mute. The radio prattled louder. Taking the knife-sharpener from the windowsill, she commenced sharpening a butter-knife. To busy her fingers, so as not to think. It did not occur to her that any of her actions might be perceived as ridiculous, absurd. Sharpening a butter knife, watching the reflection of a boy she knew nothing about sitting in her kitchen, keeping count of the minutes before she'd be due to at the Institute, to mother her employer & tend his collection of stray cats. Such timeless actions as these. A year from now, perhaps, she could be standing precisely thus, re-enacting this same dim awareness; in two years, ten years; for how much longer after that? Where was it all tending?

Watching the boy's reflection, Madame Lenoir drifted into a kind of reverie. She'd often wondered about the turns her life had taken, about what it might've been, or might not've been. The omissions, the declined opportunities. Though she herself had never wanted children. The thought of ever bearing one had disconcerted her for as long as she could remember. Yet the way this Gep blew into his tea set her mind into dispute with itself, a sudden hysterical tension, or almost, as if all *that,* her accountable existence up to this point, had simply been a staunching, a constriction of the breath – so as not to hyperventilate. Life was always, as far as she could see, threatening to do exactly that. But now, feeling this weight in her chest, its flatness pushing against the fabric of her blouse, aware, perhaps *too* aware, of standing at a kitchen sink, with some mute brooding thing invading the confined space of her own being? The morse of Gep's breathing, the short-then-long motion of the knife set in its groove…

She could feel the heat of the blade come up through the handle. It was an old sharpener, a relic, with a groove between intersecting steel rings. Every pull of the blade against the rings caused the sharpener to twist in her hand, the blade to slip. She was completely unconscious of what she was doing, sweeping the knife backward in a stalling motion, till it slipped once too often & grazed bone, slicing her thumb like butter.

Startled, she watched the blood seep from the cut; dissolve into the groove.

Qwertz

Old mariner, foam on his beard . . . . Grizzled sun in eggwhite of sky . . . . Eyes glazed against . . . . A faint evaporating drizzle . . . . Fog of it all . . . . Stink of it all . . . . Blearing out at the tide . . . . The quay . . . . That weary verge . . . . Ebb before flow . . . . QWERTZ by name . . . . KLOTZ by birth . . . . A screw-up in the Displaced Persons Registry . . . . Amerikaners at the end of the War of Wars . . . . Nib-pen-&-spectacle types . . . . When he was six . . . . Conceived at the Anschluss, in the Arschloch of Mittelevropska, our little Aryanised vagabond . . . . Jettisoned by a staff officer in rapid retreat to the banlieues . . . . *That's a lot of years, vieux con, to still be going on about it* . . . . All because with right-coloured hair . . . . The others not faring so well . . . . Not by a long shot . . . . Express to Mauthausen . . . . Well, you have to live long enough to fatten your sins before you eat them . . . . Confit of lard & a sweating bottle of Liberation Day Bordeaux filched from a cellar behind the Panthéon . . . . AUX GRANDS SALOPES LA CONNERIE RECONNAISSANTE . . . . And the dead woman on the cellar floor . . . . Facedown . . . . Nude as a naiad . . . . With an open suitcase full of Reichsmarks cuffed to left ankle . . . . Too hungry . . . . To care . . . . Stuffing his face, right there in the fetid August corpse-stink, six years undead with a gut-ache & drunk as a fart, puking all over when the partisans burst in . . . . Annus miserabilis of '44.

Qwertz jetted a stream of snot into the cup of his left hand . . . . Inspected before wiping on flagstone . . . . Coughed . . . . From where he sat the river flowed left to right . . . . A pale sun, tilting ostward, glinted in it like polished coprolite . . . . They would've sent him back, if the old lady hadn't intervened . . . . The Amerikaners, back to wherever they guessed he was from . . . . Paperwork . . . . She, growing blind in a junk-filled attic on rue Rollin, opposite the school . . . . École Élémentaire Mixte, Ville de Paris . . . . Where later they put a plaque up by the gate: *Victimes innocents de la barbarie Nazie avec la complicité active du gouvernement Vichy . . . . Ils furent exterminés dans les camps de la mort* . . . . Not him, though, the blond *petit juif* now barely at all, grey what's left of it, in tatters down his neck . . . . Remembering the green gargoyle fountain & stairs between streetlevels, apartment at the top, where she lived, the widow . . . . Place Benjamin Fondane a.k.a.

Fundoianu a.k.a. Wechsler / Wexler / Vecsler, *poète et philosophe, 1898–1944*, slow train to Auschwitz two months post-Liberation . . . . Well that's what they call justice round here, kid . . . . *Gaz à tous les étages* . . . . Every time he climbed them, the stairs, desperation by increments, thinking . . . . What? You survive to be punished . . . . Knowing, one day hungrier & you'd've eaten anything back there, in that cellar . . . . And go on with this thought, growing old while in your head that picture, forever unsullied, immaculate, gritting your teeth against . . . . Death like a beautiful piece of calligraphy . . . . Anklecuffed . . . . The left foot . . . . Death in a suitcase . . . . *Bluttgeld* . . . . He could almost taste it . . . . Almost still taste it . . . . Death's ball-&-chain caught in his throat.

The Widow Fondane, too . . . . All of them . . . . Due his turn any day now that atonement had exhausted its supplies . . . . The fear that'd driven . . . . Art, the soteriological force of . . . . Clarity . . . . The naked ever-fading light . . . . Like a man with the barrel of a gun in his mouth who has a taste for metal but no mettle to pull the trigger . . . . Haha . . . . Thinking how in time it all comes out the same anyhow . . . . Only you keep your brains inside your skull to rot instead . . . . Mealymaggotmouthed . . . . Mumbling at the river . . . . The daily ablution . . . . Bum-suit marinated in Time's liberal incontinence, spilling out through the seams . . . . As now, nursing a bottle on the Quai . . . . Upended, all done, tossed into the brown sludge of it . . . . One belch for his peerless posterity, another for . . . . He couldn't remember what the other was for . . . . Black under the claws working the knotted laces, the flaccid leather tongue . . . . Laying aside the divided soul, haha . . . . *'O sole mio!* . . . . Impastoed . . . . Rolling a pair of crust-brown woollens into eggshapes . . . . One for each craw . . . . The shoes' . . . . Shirtsleeves & trouserlegs, also rolled . . . . Smear of cobalt on lapel, brown herringbone, sketchpaper in breastpocket, a wilted clutchpencil . . . . Between thumb & forefinger, pressing down the toenails till white, then letting go . . . . Readied for their morning baptismal . . . . Cocked his knees . . . . Yellowed footsoles, put down . . . . Dunked in the barges' wake . . . . Slap & suck of the waters, etc. . . . . Easing the chafed skin . . . . Old weedbeard . . . . Hair perhaps flung in the wind . . . . Or he wore a hat? Pulled down over the oculars . . . . Some faux fedora . . . . His eyes might've been his most impressive feature . . . . One half-green, one black . . . . An annelid's window-onto-the-proverbial peering from its blindeyhole . . . . Shuttered . . . . Unshuttered . . . . Pluck out thine etceteras . . . . Wherefore? The belated earlybird choking on a braillestick . . . . *Cockatrice! Clochecall! Cocorico!* How once-upon, all the crocodile tears in the Nile wouldn't've been comfort enough . . . . He with his strawman's dry heaves making a washingmangle's music most discerning . . . . A sight to behold, as they say . . . . Treading water on dry land, in a manner of . . . . A threshing dance . . . . A lame duck's mazurka . . . .

To starboard a fisherman's dog sniffed an osse of seagull turd, très gourmand, cocking its head . . . . To port, the earlybird easel-daubers along the Quai . . . . Our Lady on her back knees up to be fucked, river tresses Ophelia-like trailing . . . . As if some septuagent Bonnard . . . . The delirious sky might piss on her . . . . Cloudless miracle . . . . Golden raiment . . . . See if they could put that in their grotty postcards . . . . The angler angling his mighty rod out over the flume . . . . To hook a drowned man, belly up . . . . Now that'd be a sight . . . . Cold working its way in, numbing his hemlock foot . . . . Imagine Christ stubbing his toe on the waves as he walked . . . . Splat . . . . Downward Qwertz glanced: still all there . . . . Splishsplash . . . . From above, laughter . . . . Qwertz massaged the stiff end of his vertebral column, turned . . . . No, not God on high having His last little joke, but a girl peering from the parapet . . . . Qwertz fingered his gums . . . . The girl's keen regarding gaze regarded him keenly . . . . Or not him but only the space around him, like a smudge on a lens . . . . Blonde . . . . Clutching a book in brown waxpaper, pages windtossed, unfurling . . . . Knitted beret . . . . Gabardine manteau . . . . Laughed again . . . . At anything . . . . Reminding of the last time, the one from rue Richard Lenoir, the downstairs bar . . . . Also blonde . . . . Bought her drinks, a cinnamon stick in something vomitously sweet . . . . She took her clothes off, for him as she would for anyone . . . . Leopard print bra, nipples long as cigar butts . . . . Standing on the bare concrete of his studio against a curtain of green plastic . . . . Crime-scene accoutrement . . . . Then a bare mattress with legs up so he could see . . . . The angry redness in place of the bush, as unto Moses . . . . He sketched pessimistically . . . . She prattled . . . . Then he prattled . . . . Old-man stories . . . . Great art, his solemn man-voice solemnly said, should help acquire an acceptance of life . . . . The charcoal fractured . . . . She could only orgasm, she'd said, having her nipples sucked . . . . He smudged he erased . . . . The word "sucked," *sucé* . . . .

In his mind, he sucked the brown nipple while the blonde barmaid, stroking an engrossed clitoris, cackled Tiresias-like . . . . He drew her that way, one hand between her legs, the other offering the bare outline of a breast to the implied observer . . . . To him . . . . To you . . . . Creature of myth . . . . To *suck* . . . . He worked till his arms & fingers ached . . . . The blonde farted, she slept, in ageless pornographic somnolence . . . . CHARTREUSE pencilled across the drapery, if it could be called drapery . . . . CADMIUM CLAIR across the cleft, etc . . . . A Madonna in polyethylene . . . . Instructions for when, after, in his model's absence, he began filling-in the outlines, completing, re-ordering, distressing, sabotaging, till he'd approached the essence of it . . . . That *thing* . . . . That wordless affirmation . . . . To say it, though, sounded more ridiculous even than it was . . . . He wondered what book the girl on the parapet was holding . . . . Something in it had made her laugh, which in turn, etc . . . . His mind, sullied with so much metaphysics, sketched a scene in which that laughter, *as if* for the first time, like the day after the hundred-&-twentieth day of Sodom... Ah! Such a story as could be told . . . . The world-weary virgins . . . . And the eternal non-part he himself played in that picture . . . . Like one of God's chewed toothpicks propping up the eyelid of the world but not of it . . . . Laughable old fuck . . . . Like a limp dick in a brothel . . . . Like a paintbrush with no bristles, blah blah blah . . . . Caught, so to speak, in flagrante delicto, in the very act of his nothingness . . . . *Nothing's ever like anything else, ol' Verdigris* . . . . L'artiste de la disparition with his dignity laid out for all to see, oh ho, *like like like* secret little dog turds adorning the pavement cracks *hahaha* . . . .

What a flattering image he had of himself when it suited him . . . . The girl on the parapet smirked, the sun smirked back at her . . . . Qwertz hunched into his coat, filing her away in that vast kopf of his till he could screw her at leisure in a scenery more to his liking . . . . Virtue rewarded . . . . Oh there was no end to the benevolence, so far as he could picture it . . . . Wiping the rag of his sleeve across his eyes, to get the slate vaguely clean, or else muddy the whole composition irreparably . . . . Not to be stuck in one place, one *image* . . . . These little daily abolitions . . . . To keep at bay the insomnias that dogged him . . . . The subtle migraine . . . . The roaring crescendo as he bent to *set it down* in solitary coitus before the spent canvas of himself . . . . Signing it, so to speak, that accomplished thing of all his inward violations, his pathetic manias, the artist in his shit-sty, with all the practiced poignance of a child's snotstain worked with a febrile wrist movement into a subtle dismemberment . . . . A barely figured braceleting of the left ankle . . . . Of that corpse in the cellar, crotch stuffed with useless money . . . . The eternal archetype . . . . Leashed to his paintbrush by that *Q* of Qwertz, like some pimp's potlach . . . . Quod errant . . . . All these years after the fact, more fully than any faith, more immemorial than any talisman . . . .

Mahnood

The terraria stood luminous & green & exquisitely fragile under the predawn meteor shower – the eastern sky faintly streaked with red & yellow entry trails like cosmic rain drifting over the watery horizon, only to dissolve in the lavender haze of daybreak. And being one of those rare "Earth Day" conjunctions meant the twin suns appeared in eclipse as they inched their way (460m/s, relatively speaking) up behind the silhouetted urban constructs & industrial haze – the lesser ("βabs") transiting the greater ("Pαp") so as to present to the naked eye the impression of a single bright G-type star. Because long ago, in that diminished memory of barely-recorded time, on the planet from which their colonist ancestors had set out – fatalistically, never to return, never themselves to arrive, or in spirit merely, in name – each period of illumination had been marked by the passage of only one visible "sun."

Standing on the observation deck of the Astronautics Institute, Sub-Commandante Lacepède Vargas gazed at the spectacle wondrously. Not because of its aesthetic influence upon him, which was negligible, but because of how astonishing it seemed that his species' most intimate apprehension of time – that most archaic synchrony in which their very minds & bodied first evolved – could once have been so utterly foreign, so *unworldly*. Then, as the composite star floated above the rim of the great glass domes, a shriek went up from the neighbouring zoological enclosures. Peacocks & blue flamingos & domino owls. Wildebeests. Marmoths & roobears. Until, with that overripe "sun" almost clear of the haze, a whole cacophony of animal sounds choked the air – as if they, too, sensed the light's mythical provenance.

Vargas meditated thus on a view which, bar the interior of the transit shuttle & endless corridors & rooms at the Inner-Space Flight Centre, would be his last of this world. He'd carry with him, he realised, this souvenir, this last impression of "home," back to a place he'd never seen, except in pictures vaguely resembling this one, with its quaint folklore spun from a probabilistic accident in the evolution of an alien celestial body – as alien & as probable as anything else in the vastness of the galaxy. For all he knew, they could've come from anywhere, one forgotten migration after another, through spacetime immemorial. Would he ever know? Would some cosmic voice speak to him on his journey, bequeathing him the Truth?

He closed his eyes. The scene hovered, faded to red, was gone. As impermanent as that. He opened his eyes again – the same picture, yet different, both there & not-there. This time tomorrow, he'd be half-a-million miles away, with only a dashboard monitor on which to observe the receding shape of Poincaré VI – if he was conscious to do so. He'd struggled for months to come to terms with having been selected for the mission he was about to attempt. Like the ancient pioneer Gargarin, alone in a capsule, beyond the reach of any recovery crew. How strange it must've been, "first human in space," floating above a world that revolved as if around a single fixed point, like a glass bead spinning at the end of an invisible string, swung from a hook far far beyond the sky – some Lagrangean doppelganger of that "heliocentric" universe Vargas' foremothers once (incredibly) so solemnly believed in.

Perhaps it was a sign, a favourable omen, this of all "days." Vargas squinted into the haze, adjusted his bodyweight from hands to cordal flippers, so as to extract from his breast pocket a battered tin of liquorice mints. He lazily fed a pale anise-flavoured disc into his mouth & sucked. A breeze gently tossed his hair – his body rocked slightly to its rhythm. High overhead, the meteor trails descended in concentric timelapse arcs, growing redder as the "sun" rose higher. The terraria gleamed. The jaundiced sky, like a chrysalis turning gradually opaque under the influence of the twin stars' radiation, hung vastly over everything.

Schönbrunn

The bums were taking up space around a bench outside one of those nonstop Arab joints. A couple of Portuguese & a black from Senegal. Schönbrunn went in & bought a bottle anyway then hunched over to the bench & asked one of the Portuguese for a cigarette. They took the hint & faded off into the night. The Senegalese went over & squatted outside the nonstop, back to the wall, eyes fixed on nothing.

Last time Schönbrunn had bothered to check his watch, it was past four already. He'd left Laborde at Place Voltaire trying a line on a couple of beat whores. Schönbrunn had better things to do. He stretched out on the bench & cracked the bottle. Napoléon, only the best. When the bottle was half-finished he ditched it & hauled himself morosely down the street. It was one of those nights. He knew that no matter how much he drank, he wouldn't get where he wanted to be. May as well just hit the sack, try again tomorrow. The eternal fracking optimist.

Schönbrunn's ex-wife owned a flat in the 11ème which he'd kept the key to. They hadn't seen each other in almost two years. Martine lived with her girlfriend in Montreuil. Schönbrunn wondered if things would've been different, if they'd had kids. Maybe she'd've left sooner, taken the kids with her. He'd've been a lousy dad no matter how you looked at it.

The apartment was on the top floor of a rat's nest that should've been condemned already when they burned the Bastille down. He trudged the five flights on autopilot. The place stank worse than usual. Plumbing in one of the jerrybuilt cans wedged between landings had overflowed during the night, spilling down the stairs. He did his best to avoid the worst of it. By the time he reached Martine's door he was almost sober, his shoes lacquered with piss, dawn turning the skylight over the stairwell morose shades of fracking grey.

The apartment wasn't much, a room with a sink, sofa-bed & shower. Kind of an upscale version of the cells at La Santé. Schönbrunn dossed down there from time to time when he couldn't be arsed with the commute. Tonight, though, he wasn't alone. When he flicked on the overhead there was already an occupant stretched out on the sofa, sawing the air. Not Martine. Schönbrunn took a closer look. Something of indeterminate sex in a ratty polyester two-piece, department store type. No-one he recognised. Schönbrunn kicked the snorer awake. The suit jerked up, fists cocked, all in a reflex, squinting into the glare. A string of drool hung pendulous from lower lip. If this was one of his ex-wife's pansy friends, she'd sunk lower than even Schönbrunn would've expected. He flipped his ID so the wanker got a good look at the shield, then hoisted his thumb at the door.

—Now get lost.

The sleeper blinked, muttered under his breath, took in the size of the cop leering at him in close-up & decided it was definitely not worth it. No sooner out the door than Schönbrunn bolted the lock, killed the light & caved-in the sofa with his weight, dead already to the world. Somewhere down the stairwell, the suit cursed.

Two hours later Schönbrunn's phone rang. It didn't stop ringing till he answered it.

—Know what time it is, detective?

—Go to hell. It's my day off.

—Your day off's just been cancelled. Jardin des Plantes. Over there, now! There's a nice fresh stiff waiting for you.

Yadlun

Lesser minds might've found greater interest in the mere digging & filling of holes than Yadlun found in the pure apprehensiveness of excavated space – of space overwhelming in its primal emptiness – like an extruded bowel, all substance evacuating into an occulted, other dimension. Such was the work of Creation, compared to which the deserts of Mongolia & the tundras of Lapland were mere landscape. Something to contemplate after the fact. The stuff of nostalgia. God, if he'd existed, would've dwelt – Yadlun was sure – among construction sites. The idea caused the old botanist a twinge of conscience, a rueful sense of faith lost, surrounded as he was by the work of determined abolition. As if Creation itself were being packed-up, bit by bit, readied for the Big Move. But then you couldn't have one, he supposed, without the other.

This had been, in germ if not yet in the substance, the focus of Yadlun's thoughts two weeks previous as he watched the newly-arrived workmen down in the courtyard proceeded to break apart what'd once been a clubhouse with a pair of sledgehammers – causing Madame Lenoir, the Institute's secretary, to pause in her minute-taking. One of a seemingly endless roster of meetings that took place in Yadlun's office – *La Grande Galerie de l'Évolution* – a.k.a. the Hexagon, so-called owing to its six-sided geometry, turret-like, jutting from the Institute's roofline with tall sash windows & vitrines stuffed with botanical *wunderkammer* alternating with bookshelves ceiling-high. It was through one of these windows, courtyard-facing, that Yadlun had been peering with his back to the conference table when the men set to work with their sledgehammers.

Madame Lenoir had looked up from her stenographer's pad at the sound of the first blow, & she later recalled thinking how frail Yadlun appeared at that moment, framed against the glass, like some blighted specimen withering in the corner of an enormous vitrine. Godemiché, assistant director & heir-presumptive, had meanwhile rambled on undisturbed about the weekly duty roster. Unwashed coffee mugs & all that. He was the kind of man who read the smallprint on principle, because he was the kind of man liable to've written it. The hardhats, unaware of the important business going on above them, had stood out on the tar-paper of the old clubhouse roof, working their sledgehammers at a widening hole they'd opened up in the middle of it – like a pair of monkeys out on a limb, so to speak, gnawing the branch they're standing on. The Institute's cats occupied the ground-floor windowsills, like an audience in an opera gallery, observing the spectacle with palpable schadenfreude.

It hadn't ended there. Within the space of those two weeks more workmen had arrived, with heavy machinery intended for digging. No explanation was forthcoming. Yadlun, staring morosely from his window, had let Madame Lenoir understand, though not in so many words, that something ought to be done to find out what it was all about, & who'd authorised it. Knowing the workings of Yadlun's mind as well as she knew the workings of the bureaucracy they were beholden to, Madame Lenoir performed the required theatrics – more Brecht than Giraudoux, admittedly – of placing precisely three phone calls to counterparts higher along the foodchain, eliciting, as convention demanded, polite obfuscation. Three, she had long come to understand, conveying a sense of All-ness that couldn't easily be refuted on either side. And as was customary, the All had declined to have its intentions examined. No-one, in short, was prepared to accept responsibility for the reconstruction work currently being initiated at the *Délégation à l'Outre-Mer, Direction des Collections*. It could only be surmised, therefore, that authorisation had come from the very top. The Minister himself, perhaps. Perhaps the President of the Republic, even. Such things were not unknown.

In which case, Madame Lenoir supposed, everything depended upon the outcome: if the Tennis Court Conspiracy – as it was soon being referred to around the Institute – turned into a fiasco, the axe would fall squarely on their own necks, & Yadlun's foremost. However, if its obscure ends were deemed to've been accomplished, if it was duly considered a success, there'd be TV crews & talking heads in two-button suits, a ribbon to be cut, a chunk of freshly-poured foundation to be inscribed, & the obligatory schoolgirl to present the President with a committee-sanctioned bouquet.

Meanwhile, in this most grey of grey zones, of indeterminacy & incompletion, with no defined objective in view, the Institute's staff could only watch & speculate & continue distractedly with the work at hand, of cataloguing the global decline & resurrection of plant species of every known type & variety – with an eye, some joked (unconvincingly), to the one that someday might transcend its assigned evolutionary status & usurp the role of humanity itself in obliterating all others. Pleasant thought. But as far as visions of world-domination extended, the Institute – its quota of monomaniacs notwithstanding – evinced, under Yadlun's direction, a resounding inertia: the world, all evidence suggested, would take care of itself; in thirty million years none of this – plants, animals, architecture – would exist anyway. Their job was simply to catalogue it.

And so it was, with a sickening sense of vindication, so to speak, that Yadlun stared glumly at his own reflection superimposed upon the chaotic scene unfolding below. For two weeks, in a type of time-lapse, he'd observed the exposed innards of the clubhouse being reduced to rubble with bits of plumbing sticking out. Then the men in their luminescent orange smocks put their heavy machinery to work, driving ten-metre piles into the ground all around the tennis court perimeter. The noise of the machinery shook the panes of the Hexagon's windows. Madame Lenoir was instructed to make further phone calls, to no avail. The Budgetary Committee, the Resource-Allocation Committee, the Oversight & Auditing Committees, the Comprehensive Review Committee, proceeded regardless, at their allotted times, as they always had, with only minor disruption. As was customary, Yadlun remained aloof, combing his beard at the window, allowing each meeting to discover its own equilibrium. Godemiché would talk, Madame Lenoir would record minutes, while the others, unless called upon to report, would invariably remain, if not attentive, at least attendant. When the secretary's egg-timer rang, the meeting would disperse &, with varying intervals for lunch, coffee, a furtive cigarette, the next would begin.

During this time, Gep silently made himself a regular fixture in the courtyard, riding at the side of the pile-driver operator, sitting there like a peg askew on a clothesline. Now & then he'd glance up at Yadlun's window, as if seeking assurance, or offering it. The machine operator felt sorry perhaps for the mute boy, sharing coffee from his thermos, half a sandwich from his lunchbox. Increasingly despondent, Yadlun watched Gep watching the operator grapple the controls with naked wonder while the coupled sections of a huge drill-bit threaded deeper into the ground, plumes of dust spraying from the shaft. A compressor thumped away monotonously.

The scene had given Yadlun an awful sense of foreboding, a sudden awareness of his own mortality. He'd attempted, fruitlessly, to explain all this to Madame Lenoir, who offered him aspirin. Had she ever truly understood him, he wondered? Or was his secretary's maternal disposition merely a kind of soporific, like warm milk doled out to a child at bedtime, to deflect from the inevitable monster under the mattress? Perhaps she'd wanted more. Disappointed, then. But all women were, weren't they? Wasn't that the way of things, the end towards which man in his quiet desperation laboured, imagining the path prepared had been for him alone & not the uttermost contrary? As he, too, a mere drone, born to its little hexagon of time & space, among all the other hexagons, from which the mind of the swarm one day drives it forth to die in some unencumbered piece of realestate where it wont stink up the machinery.

And was the end nothing but a form of means justified? And Lenoir, the sexless queen bee, patiently tending her larvae by proxy, or whatever it was she did without appearing to do anything. Like Fate. Did he believe? What difference did it make? The risk of knowing was that the end only came quicker, better to push off into the darkness & be done with it. But Yadlun, despite these meanderings of the soul, had no faith in destiny of any kind: evolution itself abhorred the idea. Yet even still, as far as could be seen, in the present situation, he – *they*, in fact, all of them – oughtn't anticipate things getting better before they got very much worse.

As in fact they did.

The proof was laid right there before them. He might almost have called it a sign, had such a word not suggested something so utterly ridiculous. But written, in any case, as upon a wall, as upon the face of the Earth, a portentous signification. That its agents assumed the form of men in hardhats & hi-vis work vest was neither here nor there, their great work was as meticulous as any Domesday Book. Unable to do otherwise, he'd watched with a sick fascination the progress of abolition. In the space of a single afternoon an excavator had scooped-out a hole from wall to wall twenty feet deep, in the middle of which it idled like a beast staking its territory. While to one side, an umpire's chair teetering on the periphery beneath a hanging staircase, like a flagrant anachronism…

Yadlun had observed the beast's unravelling intestine, the scoria spirited away by untiring conveyor belts into a secret fourth dimension, perhaps. He'd glanced despondent at Madame Lenoir. *She must think I'm absurd*, he'd thought, as if he were the only one not in the know. *It's their revenge*, he'd decided. *They've had it in for me from the start.* He should've seen it coming. What he saw instead, girded now by a hodgepodge of scaffold, were walls of dirty red brick exposed around the excavation site perimeter. Walls that appeared to extend downwards indefinitely, as if to the very Kingdom of Hades.

The end, Yadlun had finally been inclined to agree, was undoubtedly nigh.

Gep

They hid behind faces.
You never knew which ones.
Their voices spoke at you,
the way dirty raincoat men coax cats into their reach
to hang out a window by the scruff.
Do the firecracker trick.
Laugh with dribble through their teeth
as it screams writhes erupts.
The tracksuit kids who tossed a pony
down an elevator shaft.
The men in cars with sunglasses.
Anoraks dashikis hoods.
Mort pour rien!
Rienrienrien but you can't hihihihide.
When he was six behind the project they did it to him.
First the bald one, then the others.
Putting that thing there,
in his throat,
that afterwards meant he couldn't.
Dragging him through glass & dog shit.
Freak!
Hahaha.
Too 'fraid.
To go.
Back.
Hiding in the Métro.
Transit cops.
Doctor in white coat & the funny pills.
Video nurse.
Social worker playing chase round the smiley room
with fat fuckstick hanging out.
Running running running.
The park,
the animals behind fences,
courtyard with victim cats

& old broken guy
on a chair
in the sky,
blinking wet-eyed down at him
like God.

Qwertz

Qwertz lent down & picked the soiled carnation from the stairhead where someone had tossed it . . . . Straightened, threading it through the grotty buttonhole of his left lapel . . . . *Man with Carnation*: smear of cadmium red on brown . . . . Presenting quite a picture to the world, Qwertz hoiked, spat a bloody gob between his feet . . . . The sidewalk traffic eyed him sideways . . . . Burden of suspicion versus burden of? . . . . He felt like singing . . . . *Non, je ne regrette rien* . . . . Crates of old records stacked on trestles along the river wall, kids in hats filing through them . . . . Edith Piaf muralised on hanging tarpaulin – Bob Marley on a t-shirt rack – posters in cellophane . . . . Sun Ra, *Space is the Place* . . . . A guy with beat-up headphones nodded his head . . . . One day they'd wire it straight into your brain, could be nowhere & everywhere in the same nanosec . . . . Zeitgeist with antennae on . . . . Who owned the mixing-desk though? . . . . Eye-in-the-sky stuff . . . . How, despite everything, Paris always gave him, Qwertz, the impression of God staring down into his own navel . . . . Maybe like that wherever you went, Qwertz felt unqualified to say . . . . The more they kept you inside your own head, though, the less you were in the picture, he was sure of that.

Qwertz dragged the sad sack of himself across the intersection, up the footpath, through the gateway of the Jardin des Plantes no less . . . . Beyond the whited pillars stood Lamarck in ridiculous effigy . . . . Well *bonjour vieux con*, nice day for it, what? *Fondateur de la doctrine de l'Evolution* . . . . Oohlala! Which version of the Ol' Wig's immaculate self had they incarcerated in that bronze sarcophagus? The Great Prognosticator *tout seul*? . . . . The rest of the man could be thrown away, no statue for that . . . . Spared the pigeon treatment at least . . . . The crapped-upon dignitas of Knowledge's manslave . . . . As once upon, he too, Qwertz, had made avid love to eternal Zofia . . . . A Latin Quarter idiot pointing at the moon . . . . Before Algeria & all that . . . . The barricades . . . . A truncheon on the head, Boul'Mich, *Herrschaft und Knechtschaft* . . . . Been staring at his finger ever since . . . . Smear of charcoal, pigment, glue, jism, string of snot . . . . Reamed them crosseyed, all of History's cunts lined up on the canvas, the stumpy end of his wit wilting sideways . . . . They could stuff their politics where it belonged .... The war .... There was always a war going on, someplace .... Master race of button-pushers with their eternal addling machines .... More of everything ....

Well, not quite everything, eh?

Fifty years of headache, indigestion & the piles was what his loyal contribution to the cause had earned *him* .... Arbeiten arbeiten arbeiten! .... *Redeem your nonentitised self here, sunshine!* .... Making such a man of him, oh indeed, a veritable Holy Trin of triply penitented three-in-one blindman, deafman, dumbman, not to mention the little tender-is-the-night stickman-in-the-middle to comfort him in his vierzig Nächte tribulations like a furtive fuck in the hand .... Apostle of the self-sufficient high art of the masses .... The knowledge-carnal even a bum could afford were it not verboten across the 39 provinces .... Poor Lamarck .... Angels swooped down & crapped on his head & not a damned thing the wanker could do about it .... Buy a man's soul, you own his dignity .... Mortgage a man's dignity, the rest comes free.

Qwertz slouched on, in the general direction of the Ménagerie .... As on every other morning .... Man of strictly-observed habit, our Qwertz .... Shortly after opening, 7:30 a.m. .... to be exact, had the Time Keeper's cared to measure him .... The weather, though not inclement, was not propitious .... Powder-fine white dust whipped up from the path .... The lawn was covered in it .... Around the kiosk, a sudden wind upset the tables, chairs clattering to the ground, hats blown off, leaves, debris, stuff .... And just as soon the wind, too, came unhinged, the mote-in-your-eye spectacle in rewind .... Dust settled .... Qwertz, still of one piece, turned at the wallaby enclosure toward his customary arse-warming vantage under the large fig tree .... A bench, by any other name, etc .... Wooden, with three painted slats for the hindquarters, two for the back .... Presently occupied .... The culprit, swathed in a blue tracksuit a dozen sizes too large, was no-one he recognised .... Yet .... Occupational hazard, so to speak .... Qwertz approached without stealth, paid the interloper no heed, spread himself volubly on the bench .... A time-worn custom, this voluble spreading, when it came to unwanted sitters .... To discourage .... To put the message across, etc.

The interloper remained visibly unmoved .... Dispassionate, you might almost say .... Staring with queer fixity out into the park

. . . . Or space . . . . Or anywhere as far as Qwertz could determine . . . . Face set in an autistic intensity of expression . . . . Qwertz volubly rearranged, keeping the one corner of his eye on the interloper at all times . . . . To no avail . . . . A couple of wallabies ambled over to the fence & sniffed the air . . . . *Macropus rufogriseus* . . . . Sighing, Qwertz reached into his coat & brought out a crupbled paper bag . . . . From which, a handful of grain, tossed at the long-tailed rats . . . . The red-necked marsupials nosed the ground where it fell, though not without a certain apprehension . . . . Nibbled, finally . . . . Sat back on their haunches to survey their donor . . . . Nibbled again . . . . Qwertz, less ill at ease now, allowed himself a faint smirk . . . . Clicked his tongue . . . . A wallaby shook its ears, head in profile . . . . Against a field sinister . . . . Qwertz tossed another handful of seed . . . . Turned . . . . Straightened . . . . Sighed . . . .

The interloper, though, remained stubbornly unmoved . . . . Angling his back to the corner of the bench, so as to be almost facing, Qwertz, pocketing the seed bag, sized his competitor up more flagrantly now . . . . Arab, he decided . . . . Vaguely Maghrebian cast . . . . Vagrant, possibly . . . . In some kind of trance, Qwertz considered . . . . A nut, maybe . . . . Public parks had a way of attracting them . . . . Or a poet, perhaps, which more or less amounted to the same thing – come here to let the Mind wander among remote iambic vistas . . . . As once upon, old Fondane . . . . He'd almost be willing to forgive such blatant usurpation in light of sympathetic faculties & so on, of a kindred spirit, etc. . . . . An ear to pour his grief into while contemplating the vista . . . . Which in itself was admittedly unremarkable: a line of trees, the buildings of the National Botanic Institute (*Délégation à l'Outre-Mer, Direction des Collections* no less), the wallaby enclosure, much shrubbery . . . . It was those stunted macropods that'd attracted him to this particular spot in the first place . . . . Strange transplants, like him, from alien climes . . . . Theirs in place, his in time . . . . Did they sense it too? . . . . The atavistics of lost antipodes? . . . . Did they? . . . . Yearn for it as he yearned? . . . . What unspeakable intelligence lurked in their marsupial brains?

He scrutinised again the interloper's phrenology . . . . Already, if yet unconsciously, testing its contours . . . . Fitting it into the ever-evolving tableau inside his own head . . . . It was a question of arranging the elements in such a way as to *clarify* . . . . To balance, harmonise, the unevaded chaos of his inner eye . . . . Whole rooms in there, attics, hallways, *loci memoriae*, stacked with forever incompleted *pictures* . . . . All of them, the sum of his pathetic vocation, alluding back to the one primal scene . . . . No matter how random the incorporations . . . . The who, the what, the where, the when . . . . The wherefore, needless to say . . . . They all, in the profundity of final ends, mere versions, reversions, aversions of that depressing original . . . . The consummata, so to speak, of his first awakening, in the sightless gaze of that forever-nameless *femme fatale* on the cellar floor . . . . The drama of a braceletted ankle, a briefcase, blood money . . . . Death's handiwork, like some ultimate ulterior motive . . . . Whose meaning, all these years, he was still powerless to solve . . . . To advance or regress the timeframe, so as to witness *it* . . . . And to keep on witnessing it . . . .

Lenoir

Madame Lenoir re-filled the coffee pot. White gauze encincturing her thumb against the black of the pot's handle. The sting of the wound in the hiss of the pot. The coiled element. The all-too redolent aroma of coffee grounds. She closed her eyes, listening for Gep's footsteps. The idea of him, mutely stalking through the corridors, a dispossessed spirit, from alcove to alcove, a reflection in a vitrine, a pale smear of moonlight. Mothwing. The coffee pot thumped or the element thumped or something between them. Water, heat, steam, pressure, release.

Madame Lenoir opened her eyes in time to see a hand fly to her doppelganger's breast. The mirror above the sink, staring back at her avidly, as if she were a description in a novel & her reflection's eyes were probing into her head, excising bits of her. All in a flash, just like that. Like an alien thought that arrives out of nowhere – simply *arrives*. Well she'd been alone in the office first thing every morning bar Sundays for long enough & all that'd arrived out of nowhere were these flights of foolishness. And the boy, Gep. Was that him behind her?

She turned & found the room as empty as before.

The smell of the room's emptiness.

The dull subliminal buzz & flicker of the fluorescents.

Dust, cockroach bait, the slowly composting volumes weighing on the bookshelves – as if, she supposed, weighing on a mind. The smell of rotting leaves, turned earth. It was as good a place as the next, if it was a question of containment, keeping death in its place, re-cataloguing it. The Institute had been built at a time of zeal, its very fabric the stuff of raw typology. Yadlun, too, in his own modest fashion, was a Great Chainer, believer in immutable schemes of things. What did it matter if they'd never be known? She remembered him, the way he was before, a fresh-faced graduate, plaid waistcoat goatee round steelrimmed eyeglasses premature baldpatch. A shadow of what might've been. Had he become less ambiguous with time, or more?

Steam drifted from the spout of the coffee pot. Dawn turned the courtyard windows grey. Madame Lenoir set the pot to one side, switched off the stove. A moment ago she'd performed the reverse action. But could anything ever be truly undone? Once a knot, its ghost always, hanging by a thread. "Time between it & me." A moment ago: a mirror – a flash of traffic lights – white bandage against a steering wheel – the shape of a boy hunched into the passenger seat – early morning streets – the darkness – the engine subsiding into the palpable non-silence of plants – insects – sleeping animals. *They dream that they wake to another day. Saving the best for later.* (Where did that come from?) Walking from the car to the front door: key, thumb & index. The smell of the Institute wafting musty down the stairs, the creak of the boards, the boy two steps behind. Then, at the first landing, slipping away into the maze. Slipping. Away.

Down in the courtyards the cats were mewling for their breakfast, milling at the foot of Yadlun's highchair. The defender of the faith besieged in his earthworks. They'd bury him, make a fossil of his mould. The meagre phallus of him. As the tribes of unbelievers swarmed upon the Earth, uprooting the resolved paradoxes, raising an enormous pyre of mummified cats. Madame Lenoir suppressed a slightly heretical laugh & filled a bowl with milk. It wasn't good to let cats drink milk, she knew. It wasn't good to let them starve, either. The smell of iodine dismayed her as she wiped her hand across her mouth.

Godemiché

It was June, only idiots talked about the weather. Godemiché steered his bicycle between lines of stalled traffic onto the embankment, impatiently. At that time of morning & it was already stinking hot, the daily circus in full swing. He was surprised to see a homeless guy on the riverside seated at a saloon piano, greasy cords of grey hair sweeping the keys, giving a warped rendition of *Ode to Joy*, for Christ's sake.

Godemiché pedalled on past the Bibliothèque Nationale, bowtie aflutter. In a month's time he'd be vacationing at La Rochelle, far from all this, only the fish to attend to. With any luck, by the time he returned, Yadlun would be emeritus & the Institute would, by right of primogeniture – in a manner very figuratively speaking – be his. They could feed the old bastard to his cats. Godemiché gripped his handle bars, turning his knuckles white. The thought of Yadlun's impending exit made him sick with glee. No more of that taxonomic moron reinventing the proverbial wheel at each & every turning. Oh no. All it required was a final catalyst, to drive the old man's confusion naked before the world.

Well, he'd been patient, he'd laid his traps & sprung them with the dedicated aversion to haste of a veritable tortoise. And while the hare-brained imbecile was dozing away on that antique chair of his, he'd seen the finish line come inexorably into sight. It was just a matter of timing now, that final lunge at the rope, so to speak.

Coming up to the intersection, Godemiché almost missed the red light, lost in reverie. Waiting for the green man, he rehearsed the four-point agenda he intended to raise at the weekly Household Committee, scheduled for that afternoon. His theme was reform. *The elaboration, to the very end, of the necessary implications.* If Yadlun presented the face of Experience, it was to Reason that Godemiché sought to appeal. Once led, he felt confident, the others would follow. Or if not, Reason had other avenues of persuasion. He'd laid the groundwork, soon his plan would unfold like a budding thing, flawlessly accomplished, radiant even, a testament to his all-round geniality.

The lights changed, Godemiché wedged the scuffed point of his shoe into the toe-clip & pedalled on towards the grey steel arc of the rail bridge, *Chemin de Fer d'Orléans Administration*, Gare d'Austerlitz coming up on the left. Battle of the Three Emperors & all that. 1805. The nation's last bankable adventure. Dodging the earlybird tour buses on the Place Valhubert, the crowds barricading the entrance to the Jardin, bell ringing, gravel beneath his tyres, Godemiché weaved past Lanark's statue into the comforting familiar smell of dung wafting across from the animal enclosures.

Schönbrunn

A pair of Gendarmes loitered at the gates, making a show of directing the human traffic away from the Jardin. Schönbrunn pushed past them. They should've had the whole place in lock-down, instead of just waving their hands about. He could hear an ambulance pull up behind him, sirens at full pitch, guaranteed to draw even more of a crowd. What'd they want with a fracking ambulance attracting everyone's attention for? There were more Gendarmes posted at intervals through the park. A half-hearted attempt was underway to round up the visitors. It wouldn't be easy. It looked like a carnival weekend out there. Christ, didn't people have better things to do at that hour? They'd be processing till doomsday.

One of the sentries directed Schönbrunn towards the Ménagerie, some kind of mini-zoo they'd packed off from Versailles in the spirit of democracy, back in the day, for the great unwashed to get an eyeful of exotic bestiality. He saw a red panda up in a tree stroking itself while stuffing its snout with foliage. A dozen or so plainclothes had gathered nearby, apparently unconcerned by the bear, or whatever it was, avidly wanking right on top of them. He recognised a couple of eggheads from forensics. One of the crime scene photo boys came towards him. They knew each other by sight. Gilles, he remembered the guy's name was. Schönbrunn flipped the top off a pack of Gauloise & Gilles helped himself.

—Ça va?

—I've seen prettier.

—What's the gimmick?

—School teacher. Someone caved her head in before strangling her with her own underwear. Or maybe it was the other way round.

Schönbrunn pulled a lighter from his jacket pocket & snapped a flame out of it. Gilles got his cigarette burning & drew on it with determination. Exhaled.

—Long night?

—Naturally.

Schönbrunn got his own cig going & pocketed the lighter.

—It's my fracking day off.

—Too bad for you. Thanks for the fag.

Schönbrunn grunted, rolled his shoulders & headed towards the scene. He got some looks as he pushed his way in to what some college smartarse who'd come to give them a lecture once called the *nodal point*. The dead centre. A couple of the forensics boys were still busy with tweezers taking samples like it was a depilation job, everyone else just standing around massaging their paper coffee cups.

The corpse was naked, they hadn't covered it yet. It seemed to stare right up at him with its one undamaged eye. Sort of an imploring look. He tried to imagine the stiff with makeup on, after the undertakers had done their restoration work. Like some solemn & truculent Marilyn Monroe sculpted from flesh-coloured putty, blonde wig & glass eye. The mouth was half open, a couple of ants were navigating their way towards it up the right side of her face. The left side, what there was of it, was caked in blood but no ants, no flies either. Same down below. Legs bent at the knees & both slumped over to one side. The bloodied mess visible all the same. Some bright Joe must've done a half-arse job of spraying bug repellent on her to keep the creepy-crawlies off. DDT maybe. Not as if it'd contaminate the evidence. It wasn't bug repellent that killed her.

They were bringing the body-bag when Laborde sidled up beside him, reeking of five-euro cologne. Schönbrunn could feel the stubble on his own face & the wax that passed for skin underneath. Three days without a shave. Well it wasn't his job to be pretty. He dragged on his cigarette down to the butt, then stubbed it out in the dregs of Laborde's coffee. The butt hissed in the big man's paper cup – held, Schönbrunn couldn't help noticing, daintily by the fingertips, with the pinky sticking out, like it was a fracking Piña Colada. The shirt today was orange, with a zoot collar & cuffs too long for his coat sleeves. The suit needed dry cleaning. By daylight the stains were revolting, but Laborde seemed not to give a frack. Schönbrunn stuffed his fists in his pockets & watched the medics work the bodybag over the stiff, snagging a tit on the ziplock.

—So what's your take?

Laborde shrugged his heavy shoulders, dislodging the roll of fat that rested atop his shirt collar.

—Who knows. Maybe she was a whore.

—Word is she was a school teacher. Had kids.

—Whores have kids.

—Be charitable for once in your life, Laborde. Think of your own mother.

—My own mother was a whore.

—Christ, don't you have any self-respect?

—Frack that. Why d'you think I signed up in the first place? What the old lady always said, only thing for a bloke with no self-respect, is join the cops.

—Up yours.

—Sure. Maybe you can fool yourself, detective, but not me, pal. Not me.

—Up yours with spangles on.

A sudden, gut-churning scream caused everyone but the medics to turn their heads. Schönbrunn looked past Laborde in the direction of the animal enclosure. Then the scream came again. Laborde chuckled.

—Peacocks, someone said. It's goddamn peacocks.

Mahnood

The blue light revolved far away in the distance, flashing faster & faster, a blue dot growing bigger, brighter, flickering between the braches, then a screeching, a long tortured wail. And he was floating, through the airlock into the command module. Flick the switches. A warning siren. Ten minutes till launch.

Sub-Commandante Lacepède Vargas grappled his way into the cockpit. Buckled the harness. The ship-board computer was running through its subroutines. On the secondary monitor, the jetway was already retracting into the mothership. Preliminary countdown spiralled to EIGHT-MINUTES-&-COUNTING. Vargas gave the computer the code to disengage. Entered the Sagan-coordinates for Trans-Orbit Injection. The target grid on the primary console locked-on. In the crosshairs, a blue dot, barely a pixel's worth, shimmered against the black.

Vargas ramped-up the image resolution. Planet Earth. The place he'd always been taught to think of as that abstract entity people called home, but'd never been. In a thousand years, no-one had. But now the boys on "Houston" had cracked the wormhole algorithm & were sending him *back*. On a solo scout mission. Suicide mission, it sounded like. Just him & an ancient fusion-drive on a one-way trip. The blue dot blipped on the screen.

As Vargas punched the ignition & launch sequence he felt an undefined presence beside him. Ghost-in-the-cockpit stuff. The *ISS Max Ernst* shuddered. Lights flashed, the siren wailed louder. He stared at the console, at the blue dot, at the numbers spiralling backward, waiting for zero. As the boosters ignited, he heard a voice speaking to him. He tried to understand what it was saying, parse the words out of the background of Mission Control static & erupting solid fuel. A voice like whispering megatonnages. Like a fat Hendrix chord with endless replay potential.

Suddenly the weight of a dozen gravities fell on him.

He felt the musculature in his face spasm & seem to liquefy. If there were gods out there on Poincaré VI, now would've been the time to start praying to them. Vargas struggled with his eyes. A bright blue face shimmered against the instrument panel, laughing, screaming, coming apart. Then the face stretched away, twisted, spiralling like a stationary whirlpool, & Vargas realised the ship must've already fired its last stage & was already careening away through the heliopause towards the Interstellar Transfer Point – its coordinates glowed & receded on the screen, light bending in the time it took the eye to register what it was seeing. It wasn't like hyperspace in the movies at all.

The face was his, of course, reflected in his visor. It hovered there on the edge of abstraction. Once the ship hit the wormhole breach he knew time itself would appear to stop. Beyond that, the simulations were too complex to explain, other than by pure metaphor. He'd imagined it as something like being inside a beam of light refracted into billions of probability vectors then somehow, magically he thought, recomposed as if by a cosmic lens, back into the sum of himself. Somewhere in the vicinity of Earth, give or take the euphemistic standard deviation. Except that this'd only ever been done before with robots: they knew it was *possible* & that was all – none of the call signs to Earth had ever been returned.

Vargas struggled to keep conscious. The ship was still accelerating, approaching cut-off. His mind fluttered. He wanted to be awake to see it, the wormhole itself, whatever it was. Some nebulous vision of the ruins of time maybe, the birth of the galaxy. But even as these thoughts struggled to cohere, the blackness folded in around him. The instruments vanished. The sound of the blood beating in his veins stopped suddenly…

Then, just as suddenly, Vargas felt the pressure of the g-forces abate, as if he were floating, becoming weightless. Something blue glowed in the darkness. He blinked. A planet. Stars. He was floating in space, outside his ship, drifting, falling. Bits of rock & debris floated past. *What happened? Where am I?* The planet grew larger, familiar somehow. He stared at it uncomprehendingly. The moment stretched out. As the ringing in his head faded he heard a voice crackle in his earpiece. Someone from Mission Control must've been trying to get through. Vargas opened his mouth to speak, but it was impossible. The voice in his ear hissed with static. He detected laughter in the background. Music. The inside of his visor began to fog up – it wasn't supposed to do that. The planet was much closer now, a looming haze of blue.

Just as the fog obscured his view completely, the voice on the intercom cleared itself of interference. Vargas concentrated hard on it: he'd been wrong, it wasn't "Houston" after all. Whoever it was sounded very close & yet very far away at the same time – a cheerful voice, the sort of voice he knew from TV reruns. He listened closely. There was something very strange, absurd even, about what the voice was saying. Someone must've programmed it into the ship's entertainment system as a joke. Vargas sighed, he wondered how much longer this part of the voyage would go on for, before he had to prepare for re-entry manoeuvres.

He closed his eyes & let the voice prattle on, wondering if there was a visual track he could pull up later on the monitor, to see who it belonged to. *Don't be an idiot*, he told himself, *the whole thing's just a dream. You passed out at take-off.* Gradually he felt himself sinking back into his harness, then the sensation grew. He was falling now, faster & faster. It was a vaguely pleasant feeling at first, until his stomach began to turn. Something like fear gripped him. Vargas opened his eyes in panic, his helmet visor was shimmering. He gasped. The voice in his ear continued unabated. Sweat poured down his face. All of a sudden Vargas found himself struggling for breath. He felt like he was burning up. Something very bright…

—And so, the voice crackled, the mystery of the Cretaceous-Paleogene Extinction Event was finally put to rest by Sub-Commandante Lacepède Vargas of the *ISS Max Ernst*. Having accidentally exited an interstellar wormhole in the wrong time-frame, the *Max Ernst* ploughed head-on at a velocity of approx 1787.98 kilometres-per-second into a previously unknown secondary moon in orbit around the Earth, causing the satellite to explode in a massive – &, for the unsuspecting megafauna down below, catastrophic – meteor shower, thereby altering the course of planetary history. It would take another sixty-six million years, however, for the *Max Ernst*'s final transmission to be received & decoded by technicians at the Cecil B. DeMille Space Centre in New Houston – having ping-ponged across half the galaxy – on an unseasonally hot June morning, 2020 Post-Terra. *Oh shit*, it said. *It's a goddamn moon.*

Gachette

From her sentry station at the entrance to the Hexagon – between *Massacre at Montségur*'s lurid accounts of raids launched by medieval monasteries to kidnap each other's scribes, as part of the Crusade's consolidation of the lucrative book-copying trade – Madame Lenoir observed the arrival, one by one (never two together), of the Institute's staff. In a blue ledger kept in her top drawer she penned the time beside each name in turn. Gachette, their intern from the Sorbonne, had just come up the stairs, panting for breath, the rouge of her cheeks rhyming with her hair. 7:13. The girl winced at the secretary as she greeted her & proceeded directly to her workspace: a sloping desk flanked by a vertical filing cabinet on one side & front-facing window on the other. From it, the view stretched right-to-left all the way from the large glasshouse to the little kiosk, with the wallaby enclosure dead centre.

Gachette hung her coat from the back of her chair & dug a folder from her bag. She spread the folder open on the desk, checked the contents, then hesitated before tracking back across Madame Lenoir's line of vision to the coffee urn. The old woman inspired in her a certain awe whose rationale the intern would've been hard pressed to explain. As if emanating from some deeper mystique, of arcane knowledge, of unspeakable taxonomies describing occult worlds of secret initiation. Worlds that the *publicly visible world* merely served to conceal. Worlds of which only they who'd passed the Institute's threshold – & those of places like it – had the faintest inkling. She was – there was no other expression for it – *une femme au foyer*. Like a faintly purring female Cerberus.

While she poured coffee, Gachette squinted down through black-rimmed glasses at the workmen in the courtyard. One of them whistled up at her & she stepped immediately back from the window. The rustling of pages & the scratching of Madame Lenoir's pen competed with the ticking of the wall clock. A creaking floorboard alerted her to the nearby presence of the mute child who haunted the place like an unconvincing ghost. Gachette had no idea who he belonged to or why he was there, only that he could sometimes be seen slinking about the bookshelves, cat-like, peering between the books from the other side.

Madame Lenoir sometimes fed him cookies & milk, an occurrence that struck Gachette as weirdly incongruous. The Dragon Lady & Little Boy Blue. She returned to her desk & sat down, preferring not to think about any of that.

Spread out from the folder was a sheaf of xeroxed news-clippings & a case study that'd recently appeared in a Dutch journal of anthropology. With the aid of a dictionary at the Bibliothèque Nationale she'd attempted a rudimentary translation. It concerned an instance of epidermodysplasia verruciformis that'd been reported on the island of Borneo. The newsclippings, on the other hand, concerned the suicide of a young woman in Massy-Palaiseau. The woman had posted a video online. Gachette, along with several thousand others, had watched it repeatedly before the authorities had taken it down, & it haunted her, causing the only nightmares she could remember having since she'd been a child. And while the two cases appeared entirely unrelated, something inside Gachette had been drawn to a sensed commonality, which in turn pointed to what, in her own research, was as stark in its omission as a missing link in an evolutionary chain.

Epidermodysplasia verruciformis (also called Lewandowsky-Lutz dysplasia or Lutz-Lewandowsky epidermodysplasia verruciformis) was an extremely rare autosomal genetic hereditary disorder characterised by abnormal susceptibility to human papillomaviruses (HPVs) of the skin. Uncontrolled HPV infections resulted in the growth of scaly macules & papules, particularly on the hands & feet. As in the case of the Tree Man of Borneo, whose limbs had become so infected as to resemble the roots & branches of trees & whose lymphatic system, it'd been observed, had appeared to be in process of undergoing strangely *plant-like* mutations. It was almost as if…

But at that moment something caused her to look up from her notes &, missing the word to continue her line of thought, to seek it among the scenery outside her window. Gachette found herself staring at the wallaby enclosure, then at a bench adjacent to it where she caught sight of a stunted sickly-looking Arab man, gesticulating in an extremely agitated way while appearing to shout at the fenced-in animals. His mouth moved but the sealed window precluded her hearing whatever he was saying. A much older man stood nearby. There was no-one else in the vicinity. Perhaps, she thought, there was some sort of altercation going on. Or perhaps the younger man was deranged. It wouldn't've been the first time. The Jardin had a way of attracting loonies, most of them harmless, but how could anyone be sure? Gachette felt the vague unease she always felt when confronted with uncertainties that were potentially threatening. She wondered if she ought to inform Security…

And at exactly that moment the gesticulating man turned his face in the direction of her window – almost as if he'd sensed her watching him. But she couldn't see his eyes, which were dark, shadowed by his hair – though she had the strangest feeling he could see hers.

Qwertz

The interloper waved his arms . . . . Some sort of loony, Qwertz mused . . . . A manic Marcel Marceau conducting the scenery . . . . Allowing himself (Qwertz), for what it was worth, a moment's amusement at this witless Wanderbühne's expense . . . . So much for a bit of bloody peace & quiet . . . . Usually he could've killed half the day easy just sitting there listening to the trees, the wallabies munching on the grass, the pigeons crapping on the eaves of the red brick pile just over yonder . . . . Well, you can't have everything as the Widow Fondane was wont to say . . . . Drumming her alteschule homilies into that Little Lord Fontanel of his . . . . Also not so little . . . . Some lessons requiring more drumming than others . . . . A boxing in the tympanum not at all out of the question . . . . He clicked his tongue, a picture of all patience, biding his time, so to speak, till this travelling circus of a creature wound itself up sufficiently to cartwheel off to its next port of call, so to speak . . . .

Somewhere a siren wailed . . . . It wailed closer . . . . Qwertz, pivoting on his left buttock, pointed his head in the general direction . . . . East-by-northeast . . . . A rumour of blue light flickering between the vegetation . . . . Something happening behind the trees . . . . Inquisitive as he was, a half-inclination seized him to have a little looksee . . . . Never knew, eh, world being what it was . . . . And by so-doing give the nutter on his left a bit of room to build up to a proper crescendo under his own steam . . . . Opportunity presenting like that for a bit of human kindness . . . . Maybe spontaneously combust by the time he got back . . . . Wipe the bench down with a bit of the ol' *Paris Match* & good as new, a chance to start over, toss the rodents some birdseed, oblige himself to enjoy the lungtingling morning air in harmony with beauteous nature . . . .

Qwertz edged both buttocks now in unison to starboard & hauled up shoe-wise onto solid gravel . . . . He scantly regarded the interloper . . . . Wouldn't want the sinister Ishmaelite to get any sneaky ideas about reoccupation, stretch out opportunely lengthwise along the deck so as to gain a monopoly on it, etc., giving rise to necessity of disproportionate force in justified retaliation, etc., etc . . . . Better put him straight, right at the outset, give him the hard word, let him know which one of them had a demonstrable prior claim, no point windbagging after the fact was there? . . . . Qwertz drew himself up into an imposing question mark, twitched his lips, but the interloper beat him to the punch, so to speak . . . . His ungainly arms swung even more wildly, nylon flapping as in a windtunnel, eyes bugged, cheeks ballooning around a puckered knot of unhaired sinewy dark lip . . . . Qwertz grew vaguely alarmed . . . . Another siren, as if pursuing the first . . . . More of the flickering blue . . . . The interloper's face went truculent shades of Maghreb, Moorish, Moroccan, Mauretanian . . . . The difficulty of keeping one eye on each . . . . Qwertz, trapped between competing impulses, impulsively booted the interloper in the vicinity of the left kneecap . . . . Of which he realised, finding only empty tracksuit leg, there was none . . . . Nor of the right . . . . Two flapping protuberances merely, dangling over the edge, swaddled in tattered nylon, blackened, calloused, more flipper than foot . . . . Obviously some kind of deficit in the perambulatory nethers . . . .

Qwertz gasped at this flagrantly unanticipated state of affairs, stumbled back, froze, mouth stupidly ajar . . . . A series of more or less incoherent abreactions raced between cranium & corpus, bungled into one another, enlarging his stupefaction . . . . Simultaneously the cripple, too, gasped – the two extensor-like arms seized-up – eye-whites flickered . . . . Qwertz, in suspended animation, waited for what would happen next . . . . What happened was this: the cripple, after terrible moments of suspense, flung his head & arms back across the slats in a violent spasm, before deflating in on himself in a cruciform tracksuited heap . . . . The whole thing was something of an anticlimax.

It reminded of the guilty disappointment, after the War, watching those mardigras papier-mâché Hitlers, Görings, Goebbelses & Himmlers paraded through a gauntlet of jeering citizenry armed to the teeth . . . . *Schnell, mein Führer, einz zwei drei!* . . . . And when their heads exploded, wha'd'ya know? . . . . Nothing but confetti sprayed out, the cheap bastards . . . . Not like that fat-arsed fieldmarshal they'd strung up at Nuremberg, for all *that* was worth . . . . Should've strapped the sonofabitch to a ten-tonne bomb & dropped him from an aeroplane, as the Widow Fondane'd charitably said . . . . And she'd said also how, if it hadn't been for Stalin putting Berlin out of its misery, the population would've been left to die miserably from cancer of the tongue, throat, oesophagus on account of all that shiteating cocksucking arselicking

& SeigHeiling . . . . Nothing too good for the Master Race, eh? . . . .
Give 'em all shovels, as some prating wisearse once declared, *'n' let the
dead bury themselves!*

But oh it was no laughing matter, not at all . . . . Not even allowing
a little schadenfreude on the side . . . . And had he, Qwertz, so lately of
that Kindergarten of Earthly Delights, ever born a grudge? . . . . Well
he wouldn't've been human, would he? . . . . Though on account of, at
the precise historical jiffy under consideration, still five sizes too small
for his boots & barely even pottytrained, half-crapping in Krautisch,
half-pissing à la Parisienne, with knish for brains & a stunted shtetl-
schlong, hardly able to tell his prognathous from his posterior, not
to mention those winning good looks (eh old blancmange?) . . . . Oh,
he'd had the very best start in life, no arguing with that . . . . The whole
comédie misanthropique . . . . And look what a shining light he'd made
of himself . . . . The Promised People's Painter, his Qwertzness no less,
a veritable monument of a mensch, holding a gilded picture frame up
to posterity – as they were wont to say in the classics.

What did they expect him to do, get down on his grubby knees with
the threads coming undone & thank them morning noon & night for
the big opportunity? . . . . That's gratitude for you . . . . *Think I asked to be
born?* . . . . Oh dear . . . . Well what's an artist for, if not to avail himself
of the world's ridicule? . . . . Selling his sole a dozen times over for a
lifetime's supply of Gris de Payne, Auréoline, Carmine de garance,
Ombre bûlée? . . . . So as to curl yet another quim-struck quisling *Q*
around some make-believe Mama Madonna's adorated ankle? . . . .
Fibula fetishist . . . . Toiler of Tarsus . . . . How they'd made him suffer,
those hideous hieroglyphs! What more could six million stepping
stones to survived greatness expect than that? . . . . (And what'd *he*
ever had to survive, in fact, eh? . . . . A case of indigestion at someone
else's posthumous expense? . . . . A picturesque hangover plonked
in his very own primal scene? . . . . The source of all his succeeding
happiness? . . . . *Hallelujah, kid* . . . . And did he think he'd've been
better off with a punishment more befitting his crime?) . . . .

Hold yer horses mate!

Getting himself all hot & bothered just because some
hyperventilating nutcase had hijacked his favourite park bench? . . . .
What'd it be next?

Uncharacteristic, then, that – snapping out of it just as precipitously as he'd snapped into it – Qwertz, rather than recoiling from the suddenly prostrate personage of the indeed questionable interloper – reached instead, in a reflex not of his own fully cognisant self admittedly, to right the angle of the cripple's head, so as to unconstrict the breathing, as often before the elderly Widow Fondane in her armchair asleep, so as not to let asphyxiate .... Hippocratic duty to one's kind, so to speak ("sympathy" being a most deniable quantity) .... But where effectively did one draw the line? .... Of what kind, for all that, was Qwertz? .... His artist's eye beheld him thus, in stooped tableau, *la charité et son double* .... Detached, it wandered out through the space between: he as he would not've recognised himself; the other, a flummoxed unconsciousness ....

Re-gathering his wits, Qwertz appraised the cripple more fully .... *Hmmm* .... No doubt about it, head most definitely not screwed on right .... Water on the brain, by the look of it .... Skin & bones, otherwise .... Dope fiend? .... Not by appearance at least .... SDF, most prob .... Plenty about, umbrellas in doorways, cardboard châteaux by the Ponte Neuf, prime realestate .... Qwertz sniffed experimentally .... Not quite on the nose, eh, not the rotten camembert you'd expect? .... Younger than at first squint, too, as could be discerned by the only partial decay of exposed teeth .... Epileptic, were he, Qwertz, to hazard a professional diagnosis .... *Grand mal* & all that .... Or something else? .... Some other *condition*? .... Well there wasn't exactly a great deal he – creator of *barbouillages*, not men – could do about *that*, was there?

Qwertz was musing thus when a third siren drew his attention back to whatever was taking place a little way across the Jardin .... Satisfied the cripple wasn't about to kick the bucket just yet, Qwertz hunched back along the path to take a peekaboo around the bushes & see what all the fuss was about .... As he did so, the proverbial "little voice in the back of his head" urged a modicum of caution – some compulsive sixth sense if you like – Unwitting Survivor's Instinct ....

He paused at the far side of the wallaby enclosure & leant into the hedge where the path turned sharply towards the kiosk .... Slid his hat off before poking his head around, so as not to give the game away – being, as he had a faint suspicion of being, in a possibly wrong place at an increasingly likely wrong time, & having long before made it a rule not to attract unnecessary attention when it came to idiots in authority, especially idiots in uniform . . . . So intending, he managed to revolve one eye far enough past the leafage to convince himself – were it ever to've been in doubt – that surely no possible good could come of a dozen cops beating their way towards him through the undergrowth . . . .

Schönbrunn

It was one of the kids from the École Élémentaire who found the body, hidden under an oleander bush. It was in a fenced enclosure along the path to the Ménagerie. The body was of a caucasian woman in her mid-thirties, slight build, blonde. The blue dress she'd been wearing was torn in two & used to tie her arms. A pair of white panties had been stuffed into her mouth. A matching brassier hung around her neck – the assailant had used it to strangle the woman after, or perhaps before, raping her. The entire left side of the woman's face had caved in under impact from a blunt object. The initial assumption was the assailant knocked the victim unconscious before dragging her into the overgrown enclosure. Then knocked her around some more.

From the path, it was impossible to see more than a metre into the fenced wilderness. The boy had been playing hide-&-seek when he stumbled on the corpse. Schönbrunn, standing later in the same spot, noted how the sound of the animals in the Ménagerie was completely masked by the buzzing of the flies. On the other side of the fence, the animals were loud enough for an off-duty cop to find it difficult to think. It was even possible that if the woman had screamed, no-one would've heard it. The place stank, too. Animal smells mingled with the stench of death.

The kid who found the body had run & told the kiosk attendant who'd phoned it in. The kid was frantic. A group from the École were on an early morning excursion to see a fossil exhibit. They'd just come back from the glasshouse & been let loose to play along the paths. Apparently the exhibition centrepiece was an extinct fish called Holop-something, *tissue* or *tychius* maybe, immaculately preserved in striated stone. The kids had all taken turns ogling at it under a microscope. The dead woman under the oleander bush was their teacher.

Schönbrunn walked the perimeter, sluggishly taking in the details, trying unsuccessfully not to feel the pain of a hangover that was still just a work-in-progress. Laborde heaved his bulk alongside. Schönbrunn spat.

—Either the perp's long gone, he said, squinting past the glare of Laborde's shirt, or he's watching us right at this moment. Which d'you reckon it is?

—Well, Laborde yawned, she didn't do it to herself, so it's gonna be one or the other.

—You don't care, do you?

The morning sun was getting hotter. Schönbrunn put a hand up to shield his eyes, glanced back at the enclosure, the kiosk, the building behind it and the large glasshouse further on from that. He could just make out the dark green splotches of tropical leaves pressed against the panes. The place gave him the shivers. It was like some sort of hothouse triffid jungle in there just waiting to hatch out. Den Bien Phu all over again. The sort of place you could send in whole platoons & never be sure any of them'd ever come out again. Schizo treemen, cannibals, nutjobs smeared in fungus camouflaged into the overhang. If the perp'd gone to ground in there, they'd be better off torching it.

Laborde mopped the folds of his neck.

—Wanna take a look? he said.

—Nah, just tell 'em to seal it, I've got a courtesy call to make. Nothing for us here, anyhow, till forensics wrap up. Flatfoots can interview any stragglers. Why don't you ride with the stiff, see what the coroner says. We can poke about once the circus has packed off. Just don't get any ideas.

Labord's smirk barely creased his jowls.

—Sure, I promise not to lay a finger on Miss Muffet. Give my love.

Schönbrunn winced, glanced once more at the glasshouse, shrugged, then turned & slouched back in the direction of the park gates.

—Fracking day off, he groaned over his shoulder as he went. Can you believe that?

When it came to sex crimes the Prefecture had a roster of freaks they called in for the line-up like ticking boxes on an immigration form. Nothing doing. Instead, Schönbrunn took a drive over to a spaghetti joint called the Boît de Bologna. A stoolie lived upstairs, name of Rancid, on account of the exacting standards he maintained working the strip. Gender weirdo stuff. It wasn't something Schönbrunn was partial to, but he figured when it came to maintaining a business relationship it was best to keep an open mind. Besides, the freaks wanted to spread their disease among themselves, that was perfectly fine by him. For his part, Rancid figured, when it came to getting all intimate with the cops, he wasn't exactly the Folies Bergère & took what he could get. But even so, if there was a sicko working the rape scene in the 5ème, sooner than later the word would get to Rancid, & with a little gentle persuasion it'd come to Schönbrunn, as sure as shit stinks.

It was still shy of 9:00 o'clock & the Boît unsurprisingly wasn't open for business, but Rancid was, peddling his good looks & anything else he could sell to whoever the frack went in for that kind of thing this goddamn hour of the weekend.

—How the hell you expect me to make a living, Rancid snarled from under a pageboy wig, you come round here acting like a cop & it not even breakfast?

—I'll buy you a cupcake, Schönbrunn drawled, ambling up beside the stoolie, letting his car keys jangle from his little finger as he flexed his fist, a tired smile playing over his cop face. He was determined to enjoy this.

The pinched mouth & uncombed wig made Rancid look just like Schönbrunn's ex-wife with the PMTs, only his ex-wife's tits were smaller. Rancid's, he supposed, had to be fake, unless the stoolie'd been mainlining oestrogen recently. Maybe it wasn't even a wig the kid had on – he couldn't tell any more, he wasn't even sure he cared.

—You're all charm, detective, Rancid said, tossing a lock of black hair over his left ear. I bet you're a real lady-killer.

—Maybe they just didn't get the conviction to stick.

—Ha fracking ha.

—Tell me about the rape-o in the Jardin this a.m. & save the bullshit. It's supposed to be my day off. And you know how it is with cops who gotta listen to smartarse punks on their day off.

—I'm sure I feel mighty privileged you chose to spend your precious moments with me.

Schönbrunn grinned, dropped his right shoulder & let Rancid have it below the ribs. The stoolie doubled-over & puked on Schönbrunn's black Oxfords.

—Pute de merde de con! he jerked back, flicking muck off the toes of his shoes.

Rancid made short sharp gasping sounds. Then after a while he wiped his mouth with the back of his hand & straightened up, eyeing Schönbrunn through run mascara.

—Sure know how to get a girl's heart beating, don't you big boy?

—We gonna cut the Sonny & Cher routine, Schönbrunn snarled, or you wanna be made love to right here?

Rancid licked his teeth.

—Alright, he said, pushing his breasts out & spreading his hands defiantly on his hips. What am I supposed to know?

—Who.

—No-one's been saying.

—Sure about that?

—Jesus, don't I have enough to worry about?

—Give.

—Pick a name. What's so special about this one?

—I'm gonna get tired of asking.

—Okay! Okay! All I know was maybe a couple of bicots tried to gangbang a blonde behind Austerlitz. Some talk in the nonstop last night. Payback. For the kid you heroes fried in the subway last week?

—This one wasn't just raped, you faggot. First she got strangled. With her own underwear. In broad daylight. Max two hours ago. There were kids there. She was their teacher. The sonofabitch beat her fracking brains in. There's still bits of it fresh on the grass. You want to talk about payback? I'll show you *payback*…

Rancid suppressed a smirk.

—Takes all types, huh, detective?

Schönbrunn let his cop stare do the work for a while, then stepped around the pool of vomit & got close enough to smell it on the stoolie's breath.

—I want to know what the little birdies are saying & you're going to find out for me.

Rancid flinched.

—Don't fret, the cop grinned. I'll come round to see you again, Rancid baby. And when I do, Schönbrunn gave him a pat on the cheek, I want headlines.

Holoptychius

Holoptychius was a fish who lived a long time ago in a rock. He wore a green cape with purple stripes & had a friend called Denovian. Denovian played guitar & sang protest songs to hippies. Holoptychius wore plastic vampire fangs to school to scare his teacher. Denovian, who sometimes sported a tea cosy for a hat, made dog lemonade in a toilet bowl, he called it *mellow yellow*. They talked about starting a band. Holoptychius wanted to call the band Pectoral Fin. Denovian said they should call themselves The Rhipidistians, said it was more of a social statement. Holoptychius said only if they played rock songs & not that hippy crap. Denovian offered a compromise. Holoptychius said only losers, stool pigeons & other kinds of losers compromised. "Two's a crowd, kid," grinned Denovian, slipping out the door. With his plastic fangs & green cape, Holoptychius slouched off to the milk bar. There was no-one to scare except the milk bar owner who wasn't scared of Holoptychius's green cape & fangs & gave him a malted instead, on account. They called the milk bar owner The Triffid, coz he swayed when he moved around behind the counter, kinda like a walking plant. When Holoptychius finished his malted, The Triffid handed him a broom & told him to sweep out the back of the shop. He swept the shop four times a week, was how he got milkshakes on account. Usually he just posed with the broom slung low against his cape like a Fender Stratocluster & sneered into a mirror. There were mirrors along all the walls. He made fishy burps that sounded like Brian Jones puking in a swimming pool. He burped & burped but the words didn't come. "How'm I ever gonna be a big rockstar if I don't have no songs?" he moaned. Just then The Dealer wandered in off the street. "Hey fish," he said, "how's it hangin'?" "Man," said Holoptychius, "all I ever get's to sweep floors." "Stick in there kid, you'll get your break." "Sure," Holoptychius moaned, "like when I'm extinct already." The Dealer ordered a creaming soda & watched the muck froth & spew all down the sides of the glass. Sucked it down with a two-foot straw. Rolled his bony shoulders under the ratty duffelcoat he always wore. Disheartened, Holoptychius stuffed his plastic fangs in his pocket, scrunched his green-&-purple-striped cape up into a ball & slumped down on a stool, chin propped on the butt of the broom-handle. "Shit, kid," said The Dealer, "don't let it get you *down*." He tossed Holoptychius a sachet of green mulch & winked. "Smoke this, you'll see your problems ain't so big after all. Like the man sez, everybody must get stoned, *hehe*." And so he did.

Yadlun

Yadlun cast a gloomy eye at his bookshelves, arranged in vague approximation of Linnaeun taxonomies. Monandria, Diandria, Triandria, Terandria, Pentandria, Sextandria & so on to Polyandria, the Dynamics, the Adelphics, the Genesia, the Cryptogamia. Dark mahogany cabinets, a large antique clock set in a recess between Plato & Pliny-the-Younger, audibly ticking: Rousseau's *8 Letters on the Elements of Botany Addressed to Madame Delessert* (1772) wedged beneath one of its uneven feet. Arranged above it, out of harm's way, a dozen or so bound dissertations, his mind's children & their children's children, gathered in silent conclave as if in preparation for his, Yadlun's, apotheosis. "Nine men in the same bride's chamber." The sun would beam down upon him through the courtyard window, the Hexagon would illuminate, his martyrdom would rejoice in itself like the proverbial gilded lily in an imitation Caravaggio. It must come soon, he thought. They'll be getting impatient. They. Always *they*. If only his enemies would show their faces. If only he could know them in his final hour. Plotting his inevitable downfall, as his predecessors before him, in a long processional line descended from the moustachioed Guy de La Brosse, whose visage – that once commanded place of honour where the clock now stood – had long ago been melted down for its weight in bronze & sold to a boiler-maker.

He turned despondently back to the window. Below, the workmen were going through the motions of their charade. A compressor thumped. A radio whined. Despite it, he felt the introspective mood deepen. There seemed to be no escaping it these days. The world may well end, he considered, before lunchtime. What use was it peering up at the stars for a sign? One may as well gaze into arcane classifications of extinct species hoping to deduce the future course of a world from which one must necessarily be absent. Like a cat mewling up at a man in a highchair to be fed. Or a mute child, incapable even of mewling, just an inexpressive pair of eyes as if some harbinger of an underwhelming doom. It all seemed too ridiculous. As if, in the final accounting, his life's achievement, the meaning of his days, the great struggle, was to be a copyist of minor obituaries to the passing of lofty ideas, of whom barely a footnoted erratum would remain. In a fit of despair he'd sat down & begun counting them once, those words nominally his. Tallied them on an ancient oversized adding machine, patinaed with cobwebs & dust. Grey. Absorbing whatever light fell upon it like some primitive stealth weapon. He'd lost interest after a certain point. Ten thousand footnotes & was the world a better place?

In the courtyard, one of the workmen had left a red lunchbox sitting on the umpire's chair. It looked more incongruous than ever, a monument to an anomaly. A vaguely sympathetic pang stirred his intestines – the forlornness of objects had always moved him more than his own predicament. But there was no helping it, the one seemed to feed upon the other. Lines of unearthly communication had been established by means he couldn't explain between their insensate being & his barely sensate one. Some elemental force of entropy perhaps. Like the scene in the courtyard he felt himself inexorably drawn. To others it might've appeared a final act of defiance, refusing to yield, psychically barricading himself, so to speak, inside his teetering domain. Becoming a desperate fixity. Venturing forth, it seemed, merely to gaze heavenwards in the small hours among his feline retinue.

Yadlun was not unaware of how the occasions on which he slept at home – insofar as he had one – had grown steadily fewer. When he did, it was on a mattress on the floor, among the hairballs & dust & carpet lice, surrounded by boxes. Hundreds of them. Which, in a manner of speaking, he'd lived out of for decades, ever since his wife had vanished from the face of the earth, had died in a traffic accident supposedly – recycling their contents from one to another as the impulse took him, repositories of a private entropy. Mostly he lived out of his office drawer. Madame Lenoir, loyal to a fault, saw that his basic needs were met. First to arrive at the Institute in the mornings & last to leave in the evenings, save Yadlun himself, who'd keep a lamp burning in his office, pouring over The Grid, his life's work Unifying System of All Things organic & inorganic. He held vague beliefs in human photosynthesis, experimenting as his illustrious forebears before him upon his own person. Subsisting on no more than a few hours sleep, reclined on a daybed or on a bench in the boiler room come November, drawing upon its heat. And without fail, each four a.m., perched on his umpire's chair in the courtyard, to survey the heavens through a pair of trifocals. The vast constellated grid was like a metaphor for all he believed in, all he'd sought to achieve or know, all he doubted.

And as if summoned by his thoughts, Madame Lenoir at that very moment appeared in the doorway, resolving from the gloom of the outer office with a stenographer's pad in one hand, thin pale body moving indeterminately beneath her dress. A mannequin on wheels. A certain Monsieur Blek, she said, had telephoned from the Ministry. Monsieur Blek wished to discuss some triplicates that'd been flagged up by the internal audit. Yadlun blinked at her. Once upon a time he'd been described as a man of stark intuitions. He sensed more than saw the machinations of institutional power surrounding him. The Directorship hadn't come to him easily, but as a conclusion foregone only when all others – all options, all avenues – had come to nothing. But now he blinked at his secretary with uncomprehending eyes in which fear stood darkly naked seeking the light. If she noticed, Madame Lenoir pretended not to. Had she wished to, she could've explained everything. About the forms. About the signature so obviously forged, his, Yadlun's, in Godemiché's hand. About the impending conspiracy. But she didn't. Madame Lenoir, if not a fatalist, believed that giving a man enough rope could be tantamount to hanging him. It wasn't, however, Yadlun she desired to hang, quite the contrary. Had he known of the conspiracy, he might only have fashioned his own demise more thoroughly to abet it. Madame Lenoir was clearly able to recognise a man in his hour of need & allowed herself to be needed.

Yet Yadlun felt hopeless beneath her gaze. He stared at his hands. Then at the withered Venus flytrap that sat mouldering in a red plastic plant-pot beside the pen-set his colleagues had begrudgingly given him on his seventieth birthday. There'd been talk of a festschrift but in the end nothing came of it. After a week the plant's leaves had turned black & wilted, which remained their permanent condition from then on. A thick carpet of dead flies covered the soil at its base. This, too, Madame Lenoir could've explained for she'd witnessed its murder with her own eyes: Godemiché spilling a sachet of weedkiller from his shirt-cuff. But Yadlun refused to part with it. Its sepulchral presence in pride of place on his desk supplied, Madame Lenoir suspected, much-wanted dignity to his own decline. And produced among his enemies a certain awkwardness. As if they'd been caught, *in flagrante delicto*, plotting to rob a dead man of his grave.

Gep

What he remembered of the Other Place
was a room with a rubber ceiling.
Gaps were visible where the rubber seam
had come unstuck from the wall.
When he looked up,
he'd been able to see shapes in a black distance.
Sometimes they moved.
The things behind the rubber ceiling
evoked things under the rubber sheet
that covered his bed.
He'd wake up in a sea of piss
clinging to the edges,
the rubber thrumming as his heart raced
& the Fear got into him.
He was more afraid of the Fear
& the things under the rubber sheet
than of the cold wet.
Night visions of drowning in a desert,
rubber dunes undulating beneath tidal waves of yellow.
Riders on camel-back,
magic carpets,
oasis pelicans
all watching as he floundered & went under,
gurgling down into the depths of his shame.
The Monitor at six o'clock coming to beat him.
Something gnarled,
knotted,
as unforgiving as a length of briny rope.
And he'd wake up screaming
till the blows knocked him out.

Mahnood

Mahnood blinked at the sky, dark faced with darker observing eyes, physically bug-like, a stalk surmounted by a pair of insect monitors, the very portrait of a questionable character. The sky was pale blue, untrammelled. From Mahnood's vantage between the wallaby enclosure & the children's playground, an unobstructed view presented itself of the glass-domed pavilion, pigeons flocking above, wheeling down through constructed wilderness to the clutter of brick along rue Cuvier.

Among which, at that moment, a dark-haired woman could be seen seated behind a first floor window, dirty white shutters framing it, watching him. The way people always watched him when he wasn't looking. Black-rimmed glasses, orange pullover, hands resting at the edge of a keyboard most likely, computer screen just visible on the left glowing like an aquarium. Their eyes meeting startled her, the burden of suspicion versus the burden of guilt. Seeing what? The self-examined, self-flagellated dwarf that hid inside his head, in a different spacetime continuum from all this?

—Not everything what it seems, he muttered.

To himself, to nobody, to the ghost beside him.

The ghost muttered something back in pre-linguistic treeman babble.

He'd awoken, not in his familiar place behind the glasshouse, the one he'd staked a claim to as soon as the spring thaw set in & kept nightly possession of during the four unlikely months since, but a different one. A part of Jardin he'd never ventured before. The unease of not knowing how he'd arrived there. Wrong time-travel coordinates, perhaps? The ghost appeared to nod.

Ordinarily, during daylight hours, Mahnood made himself as invisible as possible, venturing only onto isolated benches, like this one, watching, awaiting the signs. The regular bums usually kept their distance. Something about him, vaguely manic cast of eye, shiv down the empty-trouser-leg stuff. Not suspecting what went on inside that skull of his. Calculating, down to the last piece of gravel, teleport logistics for a scaled replica of the entire Jardin de Plantes to the frozen wastes of Poincaré VI by quantum mind-control, factored to an eighteen-digit recurring decimal. Twice daily he rotated among the bins for morsels of takeaway foodstuffs. It appeared in no way strange to him that even under such circumstances he alone on this Earth was appraised of the incredible secret of the *Max Ernst.*

He smiled, exposing rotten teeth, the air stinging his gums. The woman in the window abruptly turned away, recomposing herself in profile. And if now, he thought, something were to fall from the sky? An iridium rock, dislodged from the asteroid belt, megatonnages ripping through stratosphere. The woman in the window turned to cameo: an x-ray silhouette photo-fixed on a wall.

Like Hiroshima. The Extinction Event.

Picturing somewhere, a cave or cliff, the raging tyrannosaur, pterodactyl in mid-flight, like cinema, shadows fossilised in wet sheets of photo-lithography, but who would ever see them for what they were? Perhaps shamans of the Magdalenian had read the signs, traced in ochre. Preserved an oracle out of space junk, to this day hidden deep in the ground ticking away its half-lives.

Mahnood solemnly brought his hands up in front of his face, thumb to opposing index finger, making a frame around the woman in the window. Click. Right now, he thought, she's trying to make sense of some plant DNA sequence that's totally out of whack, dug from a Mexican crater, unsuspecting of it's true import. Face to face, perhaps, with the missing link. Something from the *Max Ernst* to throw the whole of evolutionary theory into tailspin. The drama begins, mounting to the inevitable climax. He paused the film in his head & glanced around. A wallaby stood nearby munching grass behind the fence. It looked like a giant marsupial rat. Rats from space, he thought. A secret rat experiment sixty-six million years ago. Mahnood's smile distended into something that made the wallaby stand erect, its glass eye fixing on him, unwavering.

Sub-Commandante Lacepède Vargas must've hit the eject button just in time, falling to Earth with moon debris, bits of wreckage for a heatshield, skydiving down into Saharan swamp like a DNA atom bomb. Mahnood pictured him, dangling in his scarred spacesuit, psychedelic chute snagged in the upper branches of mangroves, the steaming waters lapping his silver bootees as he raises his visor & takes his first breath of the rich nitrogenated atmosphere. Some dumbstruck pigmy-like creature staring up from a tangle of mangrove roots at the fallen god…

It was only then that Mahnood realised there really was someone else in the picture, barely an arm's length away, rooted beside the bench. Not a ghost after all, or some mental emissary from Poincaré VI, or a Precambrian treeman, but a flesh-&-blood 20th-century Earthling in brown herringbone & dungarees. He caught its reflection first in the wallaby's eye. Very keen sight those creatures have, in fact not what they seemed at all, but extradimensional time-hoppers, capable of hologrammic projection, quantum voodoo, etc. Mahnood winked knowingly at the rattoid creature. It twitched its ears, sniffed, rocked back on its haunches in alarm. The Earthling, too, seemed to hesitate in the midst of some ill-defined action, one hand groping in front while its head turned in the opposite direction, squinting over its shoulder, clicking its tongue apprehensively…

Vargas, meanwhile, fumbled at his harness. The branches swayed. Something hooted through the mangroves. It hooted again, coming closer.

Gachette

Persistent Genital Arousal Disorder (PGAD) or Persistent Sexual Arousal Syndrome (PSAS) wasn't listed in the Diagnostic & Statistical Manual of Mental Disorders, vol. IV, that Gachette had consulted at the Bibliothèque Nationale, but only in volume V, which section she'd duly xeroxed & was now perusing at her desk by the window. With a yellow fluorescent marker she highlighted passages of potential interest: conflicting definitions, assumed pathology, case studies, etc. Then she turned to the newspaper clippings which, in counterpoint to the medical literature, charted the public life of an illness otherwise barely acknowledged to exist, with all the prurience & guile you'd expect of the tabloid press.

PGAD or PSAS designated a chronic overstimulation of the genital area, a purely physiological arousal without corresponding psycho-sexual arousal, not to be confused with nymphomania. According to diagnostics, the sufferer would spontaneously succumb, hours, days, weeks, sometimes years at a time, to an excruciatingly constant state of hypersensitivity, causing distress, trauma, shame, incapacitation, & depression. In a bid to exhaust or deaden the arousal, the sufferer would frequently recourse to attritional forms of masturbation. Each achieved orgasm might simply presage the Sisyphean labour of the next, flayed genitals becoming their own torture instrument. The allegory was an instructive one.

What first attracted her attention to the idea was a story buried among the back pages of *Figaro* a year before, about a suicide in Massy-Palaiseau. The victim was a young suburban housewife, divorced. She'd posted a video on the internet. *The arousal doesn't let up*, the woman had explained matter-of-factly to the camera. *It doesn't subside. It doesn't relent. You can't get to sleep. You think you're going to have a heart attack. You think you're going to die… Men don't understand it. They don't care. They think it's hot. You want tell them, "Imagine having an erection that doesn't go down, that feeling of just before you come, all day, all night, no matter how many times, no matter how much you've destroyed the skin on your penis."*

Gachette had listened to it over & over again, it gave her the creeps, but somewhere in the darkness of her own mind a light came on. A red pinprick of light that grew larger & larger till she knew what'd been eluding her in her studies, something which would cause her colleagues no end of indigestion once the implications became clear. *There were twenty-four sexual classifications in the Linnaean system, what if…*

She scribbled furiously in her notebook. In tandem with the case of the Tree Man of Borneo, PGAD/PSAS conceivably might, she believed, make sense of a condition recently observed among certain communities of *Dionaea muscipula*, a rhizomic swamp-dwelling plant native to North Carolina – possibly linked, so at least rumour had it, with experiments underway at Monsanto's Duke University lab on electroporation – which meant they'd been growing electric circuits inside plants. It also happened to be her dissertation topic, which she was currently in process of revising into a monograph – unassumingly entitled *A Study in Transgenic Cybernetics, Mutational Hyper-Sexuality & Xylomimetics*. But the problems it'd begun to pose were something greater than the sum of its parts. *Where was life going? Where had it come from? What common destiny ruled over it?* Such questions, she realised, required the pursuit of a line of research no-one had yet advanced. A line that wasn't even a line but a jumble of intuitions, leaps of faith, constellations of unlikely facts that even the most sanguine botanist might easily construe as irresponsible if not downright irrational. It made her sick with apprehension, yet all the more determined. She'd go where none had dared, none had imagined. She'd assemble all necessary proof, if only…

But Gachette's note-taking was interrupted once more, this time by the arrival of Godemiché, who'd immediately set about making his presence felt around the Institute: ostentatiously re-arranging the schedules on the notice boards, issuing voluble directives into the telephone & addressing pedantic observations to whoever happened to be in earshot, with the notable exception of Madame Lenoir, to whom he remained scrupulously deferential. Such undisguised sucking-up to the old woman made Gachette want to puke. Godemiché noticed her look & smirked back sarcastically across the office.

—How's our pretty intern coming along with her project, then?

Schönbrunn

The woman's name was Françoise X, she was twenty-eight, 5'4", blonde, unmarried, been a primary school teacher five years. Commuted to work from out past the Bois. She was described as dedicated to the kids, no one'd had any complaints on that score. The headmaster had thought she dressed a little, how do you say, *inappropriately* on occasion. Skirt a little too short threatening to expose the knees, sweater a little too tight above the midriff, for the old queer's liking. Schönbrunn figured the headmaster got the occasional stiff cock on account of the deceased & was diligently giving the impression she'd got her just desserts. Maybe even a touch jealous of the perp. Looked like the type to go home & slap the boyfriend around a bit on that account. Schönbrunn would've liked to drag the prick down to the coroner's & watch him puke all over his tie. He pictured the corpse. White cotton stuffed in her mouth, sort of old school, teenage Brigit Bardot accoutrement. Which by *his* reckoning was about as unarousing as you could get on an adult female of the species, barring polka dots & a frilly gusset. But what'd *he* know? In all likelihood your average headmaster's wet dream. The old queer was alibied, though. They always were.

—Word has it, Laborde smirked while scanning the report, that a certain candidate for the Elysée has just been fingered for making a chambermaid straddle his face & – the word the magistrate apparently used was *micturate* – through a pair of cotton panties, you know the ones, virtually identical to our sweetheart's, which the accused apparently brought with him for that express purpose & made her put on.

—Well that kills my vote right there, Schönbrunn said.

—Only problem is he's alibied for the Jardin snuff.

Laborde planted his arse on an available swivel-chair, almost bending it out of shape. The metal groaned.

—The chambermaid also alleged that he stuck his tongue in her mouth & made her suck it.

—Jesus, Schönbrunn threw a glance sidelong at Laborde, you're gonna ruin my appetite.

—Be like sucking a barbed-wire enema.

—The hell d'you dream up stuff like that?

—I guess kebab's out of the question now, eh? You wanna go grab a burger?

—Screw that Yankee crap.

—Flan it is, so. Ma Baker, she sure knows how to cook a flan…

—Which hotel was it?

—…?

—The chambermaid…

—Frack do I care? They're all the same, anyway. Stink of KY & aerosol.

—Man, you're all class.

—With spangles on, pal. With spangles on…

Schönbrunn grabbed his jacket off the chair-back & stuck an arm in it, dislodging a stack of paperwork from the usual office entropy that sifted around on his desk. A dozen case files that'd piled up from last week, beside another dozen from the week before. A sea of identical desks in identical low-partition cubicles spread out on either side, cop-talk & telephone buzz making the standard background noise. A couple of interview rooms with windows at the far end – desks in there, too. Nothing, he figured, ever got solved at a desk. Nothing got solved period. Your average case was either open-&-shut from the start, or it wasn't. People turned up dead. Someone got fingered. Someone else confessed. *You live by the clock, you die by the clock.* Hell, you died anyway.

The two detectives pushed out through the swing-doors into a corridor where a couple of overalls were drilling holes in a wall. Part of the ever-ongoing expansion of the nation's crime-fighting facilities. Down a flight of stairs & out the fuckwits' entrance onto the street. Scum drifting around the doorway, waiting for something, like they were waiting for a handout.

Ma Baker's was a block & a half from the Station, the only clients were cops or the type of people'd given up caring who they had to stand in line with. Ma Baker sold the best stale flan in all of Paris & the only coffee that could cut it. Laborde ordered two of each while Schönbrunn took up position on a stool behind a potted plastic tree that shielded him from a view of the curb crawlers.

—We gonna go & grill any of those tree-lovers at the Jardin? Laborde said, dropping his weight onto a creaky stool.

The flan looked like hundred-year-old aspic blackened on top. The coffee smelled like an arson scene after the fire crews had been at work.

—Got anything better to do?

—You're kidding, Leborde stuffed some of the rubbery yellow custard in his mouth.

Schönbrunn stirred his coffee unenthusiastically. The spoon came up coated in grits hard as iron filings. Whoever'd ground the roast must've used a sledgehammer.

—Coroner say anything worth hearing?

—Funny you should ask, Leborde chewed. They're running tests but nothing, er, conclusive so far. Said the victim got knocked around pretty good. Time of death: between approximately eight o'clock, when she let the kids off the leash, & 8:15, when they found her. Cause confirmed as strangulation. Postmortem blunt force trauma to the head. No weapon found. Found rust-flakes embedded in the back of her brain, but…

—Rust-flakes?

—Yep, it's the way of the world, pal, standards just keep on slipping, construction gear ain't what it used to be.

—Help me.

—Coroner has his heart set on the idea it was a piece of scaffold.

—Why not just a regular bit of lead pipe?

—Galvanised steel. And something about joint-pins leaving an indentation in the skull.

—I don't like it.

—Tell Strasbourg.

—I mean, why'd a rape-o drag a chunk of scaffold around the Jardin first thing in the a.m.?

—Coz he nicked it from a construction site, figured it'd come in handy playing whackamole in the park while taking his early morning constitutional? Which you've gotta admit represents a brilliant piece of foresight, from a certain, er, perspective…

—That's some stunning detective work. And did the coroner have any hotshot theories about which construction site, exactly, that might've been?

—You mean, apart from the one just short of a duck's fart from the scene? If you measured a line straight through that giant rat enclosure?

—Kidding?

—Why'd I do such a thing?

—Beats the shit outta me.

—Aw. Well, chief, it just happens they're building some sorta hole in the ground up behind that kiosk where the guy phoned-in from. Right? Supposed to be a museum there or something. Hole's big enough to dump half of Les Bosquets with pink ribbons. Scaffolds up the wazoo. Shithead could've sleazed in, glommed some hardware, cased the scene, no sweat. Christ, he could've been camping under the steelworks for a week & who'd know? The lab boys are over there now, doing their voodoo thing…

—Secretor?

—Well now, padre, that's the thing. Coroner didn't find *nada* with DNA on board. 'Course, the perp could've rubbered-up, though it'd take Houdini to get into one of those things in the time available to pull a stunt like that.

—I'd've thought you'd manage it regularly.

—Funny guy.

—Maybe he just didn't squirt.

Leborde looked uncertainly at his flan. The colour of it almost matched his suit.

—Maybe it wasn't a rape-o at all.

Schöbrunn shook his head, raised the coffee cup & tried not to gag on the mixture as it gouged the back of his throat.

—What're you telling me, she was cherry?

—Nah, nothing like that…

—Coz what I'm thinking is, the perp snuffed her with the undergarments, stowed her in the bushes, then had a flash of genius, went back to finish the job after…

—That's a long fifteen minutes, pal. Too much rigmarole.

Leborde's breath reeked. Schönbrunn batted the air but only made it worse.

—Not if the guy's a fracking psycho. He gritted his teeth around the words. Or smarter than we think.

—I don't see it. Too many holes…

—Or a lot dumber than we think. Maybe the whole thing was a frack-up. Guy didn't intend homicide, just a little mood music under the tress, except the melodymaker wouldn't spout sweet on cue, so he goes the full Quadrophenia. Pete Townshend stuff.

Fracking bezerk in other words.

He was gritting his teeth still when Leborde mashed his fist into his flan, leering sickly into Schönbrunn's face. Blobs of flan clung to his shirtfront.

—Ectoplasm!

Schönbrunn gave his partner the look.

—Ecto-what?

—Coroner's very words. No DNA, no lesions, nowhere, one, two *or* three. Just Little Bow Peep's head caved-in with the hardware, to top off the lingerie show. And *ectoplasm*. Didn't have any other way to describe it. Didn't know what it *was*, only that she was covered in the stuff. Like maybe something went splat in the middle of the headline act. Alien or something. Spirit medium stuff.

—Christ's sake, d'you make this shit up just to ruin my coffee? Because that takes some doing in a joint like this.

—Nope. Scouts' honour.

—I ain't holding any soap, you might've noticed.

—The Scouts are decent people. Don't say things like that about the Scouts.

Schönbrunn shook his head. Sighed.

—So the perp's got some kinda hard-on for construction gear & slime, is what you're saying?

—Maybe it was *something else…*

—Bullshit.

—You just haven't considered the angles, pal. Like maybe the perp couldn't get it up in the first place. Maybe he was a limpdick *and* wacko. Or hell, maybe it was a fracking bulldyke with a chip about the old school days. But maybe, just maybe, it wasn't any kind of rape o at all, just we're supposed to think it is.

—Yeah, *symbolic* you mean? Tie victim with own underwear, cave head in with metal pole, pour slime. What's that called in the textbook, *substitution fantasy* or something? Someone's sending us a message, you think? Tell me, did you try your theory on the coroner? Did he tell you he thought you were a fracking genius?

—What I mean is, maybe it *started out* as a rape-o, or maybe it didn't, but whatever it was it got interrupted *by something else.* Maybe there *is no* perp. Maybe the perp got *zapped* in the act. By aliens. Maybe.

Schönbrunn stared at the insane grin plastered across Laborde's face, then at the blobs of flan hanging from his partner's shirtfront. *Jesus*, he thought, *the fracker's madder than I thought*. And then an appalling idea occurred to him. What if Laborde suddenly just snapped, decided to pull his piece right then & there, & start shooting up the joint? Would he, Schönbrunn, lift a finger to stop him? There was no such thing as innocence in this world – twenty years being a city cop had taught him that much at least. Empty a dozen live rounds into any given pâtisserie in the neighbourhood & you were bound to take out at least one degenerate criminal sonofabitch who deserved to be gunned down in cold blood. Even a cop joint like Ma Baker's. The rest you could count as *potentials*. How the world divided up, almost as if nature demanded it: scum & potential scum. Your average cop was no different. But even so, how could he be sure he wouldn't?

—I hope, Laborde leered at him across his ruined flan with unwaning intensity, you're not thinking what I think you're thinking.

Schönbrunn blinked. The muscle under his right eye twitched ever so slightly. He blinked again. His face became still.

Holoptychius

Fishboy wound up peddling dope in the Projects, just like The Dealer knew he would. He'd sit out on a busted bit of playground fence listening to ratty old cassette tapes on a stoneage Sony Walkman one of the Project kids had swapped him, waiting for the business to rock up. He was the only peddler anyone knew who arrived early, like he was the one hungry for a fix & not the kids, which in a manner of speaking was true. He even had the sales pitch down to a fine art, like the product wasn't already selling itself. Let it be known he was only in the biz on a short-term basis while he searched for renewed creativity, him being an incog rockstar on the down-&-out, or the up-&-up, depending on how he was inclined to spin it at any given time of day. If his audience listened wide-eyed, it was only because of the brainshock – most of the kids pegged him as just some strung-out white dude they'd've put a shiv in if they could figure where he kept his stash. He'd given up the cape & fangs act for a pair of ratty suede platforms, a hammered steel codpiece, & a red bomberjacket with THE SYNDICATE stitched on the back in what once had been silver thread. Short for Deep Space Syndicate, he said to whoever asked, the name of his band before he'd broke them up *in disgust at their own success* to focus on a solo career. None of the kids'd ever heard of them, of course. He played the old-timer card, said how way back when they were causing waves they'd called themselves Deep Space Jihadis. Fame made them THE SYNDICATE, it was a statement about the System, the corrupting $, the art of Compromise. A full-blown junk addiction had etched his face into a hell-&-back ghoul mask, which let him pull off lame shit like that in front of ten-year-old kids who only wanted to score & get high & upend trashcans for entertainment. Said *yeah man, it was intense.* How, back in the long hot summer of the 3rd Intermediate, the Jihadis had scored a mega hit with "Bagdoody Blowback." He'd played a rainbow Zoot Gibson through a fuzz box for the opening riff. The sound was described by critics as "out of this world." They'd followed it up with timeless, status-quo-destroying tracks like "Carp Head Restitution," "Age of Aquarium," "Dinosaur Bong" & "Ain't no Moon" on their bestselling album, *Rockit to Death.* It'd gone triple platinum within the first week

& earned him an Everest-size mountain of blow. *Man, you coulda skied it*. And if the kids were still listening, he'd spiel 'em the whole sad epic about how it'd all gone downhill from there. The band's infighting, the record label's cop-out, the scummy manager who'd ripped them off for countless millions in unpaid royalties, the scheming wives, always someone filching his best licks before he'd even laid 'em down. *Like the whole universe was conspiring against me personally, man.* The Dealer said he shoulda had a career lipsyncing bullshit, said he looked like Captain Beefheart fucked Johnny Thunders & gave birth to a manfish, said "Hey dude, don't get so down, don't you know you're the biggest sack of garbaggio this side of nowhere?" He tossed Holoptychius a pair of Reeboks from MaxSportif. "You oughta try being less conspicuous. Blend in more. Take up jogging. You know, it'd give you a new angle, expand your market. You could pose about as some sorta lifestyle guru or something, sell to them vanilla chicks like to work on their cardio in the Bois." He flashed his orthodontics at the fish. Could already picture the jerk with a Björn Borg headband & sponsored trackwear beating the pavement in the wake of some spandex blonde, wheezing his guts out when he wasn't honing a line about being an ex-TV disco queen, back in the day, just trying to make an honest comeback is all. Hell, if the dumb fish played his cards right he might even get himself laid, nothing vanilla chicks go for faster nowadays than one of them *Down & Out in Beverly Hills* types, hehehe, thinking how groovy it'd be to turn on with a real authentic has-been pulling out the ABBA moves. "Dig it bro," he winked at the fish, "you could stick little mirrors on your fishballs & hypnotise 'em while they do lines off that shrivelled junky fishdick of yours. Build up a real loyal clientele that way, hehehe." Holoptychius, who could see his predicament all too plainly himself, stared glumly back.

Qwertz

There was no difficulty recognising the shape & meaning of the mob as it approached from the direction of the kiosk . . . . Until that moment, he'd managed to take in the spectacle of the police cordon miraculously unobserved . . . . Their malevolent determined choreography possessed all the hallmarks of something untoward, scything with batons at half-tilt, heads down, gazes fixed . . . . Searching, obviously, with no apparent luck . . . . Qwertz vaguely suppressed less vague intimations of schadenfreude . . . . The cops beat about the bushes for longer than seemed feasible before swinging about in a line & beating back the way they'd come, clearing a parallel swathe down the side of the Ménagerie . . . . He supposed there was some sort of pattern to it, the forensic cop-mind at work marking off grids on a crimescene map . . . . He wondered what it was they were looking for . . . .

Curious, he'd edged out into the open for a better view & that was a mistake . . . . First he heard the shout, then, past the hedges bordering the kiosk, saw heads begin to turn . . . . Obviously, he thought, something'd happened & the cops'd started rounding up whoever happened to be in the vicinity . . . . And now he'd been spotted, too – immediately scenes flashed through his head: *Eh, you!* Ordered to hand over his ID . . . . *What sort of name's Quirts?* . . . . Forced to take his turn with the other unfortunates, answering the usual cop questions posed with all the finesse only cops were capable of . . . . *Not born here, eh?* As a theme, it didn't show too much promise . . . . L'interrogation de l'artiste . . . . *Oh, you're an artiste, eh? Make lots of money doing that, do you?* And there he was, again, creating an exception of himself, as if anyone gave two fractions of a toss . . . . He'd been doing it all his life, he realised . . . . First the War, then after, de Gaulle, Algeria, the FLN, '68, & every other opportunity since, that unerring instinct for being caught on the sidelines where he shouldn't be, hahafuckingha . . . . Now at least he looked the part, old bum in ancient herringbone, still didn't stop them swinging a truncheon headwise if they could get within reach, even just for the crime of easing his calloused arse on a bench to take in whatever scenery was still available to the general public . . . . *What reason did you have for being in X place at Y hour?* . . . .

Want to watch what you say, mein Freund, or they might break your hands as well .... Better just to be a bum with your brain eaten by turps, at least you get to play dumb ....

—Oi, there 'e 'is!

Qwertz hesitated .... He was absolutely sure now the voice was referring to him .... Caught *in flagrante delicto* with his eyes hanging out, as they say .... *Eh, you! Come 'ere .... What's the idea, sneakin' around in the bushes?* .... The sirens meanwhile had stopped .... All had gone quiet in the wallaby enclosure .... A general paranoiac silence descended over everything .... Qwertz began to sweat .... Nothing he could do now, it appeared, without attracting further suspicion, whether he tried drifting surreptitiously off or gave himself up, so to speak ....

Past the kiosk, men in white coats wheeled a stretcher onto the footpath .... The mob parted to make room for it, like a scene by Géricault .... Then another shout & once more faces turned .... Qwertz didn't hesitate this time but beat a precipitous retreat .... His accidental companion was sitting where he'd left him on the bench, conscious now at least, muttering looneybin gobbledegook, to himself or anyone (invisible presences, who'd know?), a brainshocked look on his face .... Qwertz grabbed him by the sleeve & shook him hard .... *Wakey, wakey! Hand off snakey!*

—Looks like trouble, kid .... We'd better scoot ....

He could hear the commotion growing in the insufficient distance .... The rest was reflex, atavism of the boulevards wired into the backbrain .... Qwertz, old man that he was, dragged the cripple off the bench .... As fast as he could, which wasn't very, he made for the bamboo beside the red brick pile, Institute of Something, his charitable burden dragged at arm's length behind .... A face up above in a window regarded the whole undertaking impassively .... Qwertz spotted it .... *Gott in Himmel, they're everywhere,* he thought .... *There's no escape ....*

—SCHNELL! he screeched.

The dysplasiac flapped in his wake, casting bewildered looks, a swimmer among men .... If they made it into the greenery, he'd be better off swinging from branches, vines, anything .... The mob meanwhile had broken free of the cordon, shouting, pointing, gesticulating, growing larger it seemed, spreading out from under the trees towards the two escapees like a pool of malevolent piss . . . . From some buried part of Qwertz's mind they screamed, *Juden raus!*

—BOLT! he yelled in the cripple's ear . . . . OR THEY'LL TEAR US LIMB FROM LIMB!

Dark calligrammes in uniform now too . . . . Was he awake or dreaming? They'd come, bashing on the door, to send 'em back where they belonged in their shtetls . . . . Even so long ago, barely knee-high in his socks, there'd been no doubting the mob's mood, its blood frenzy – the air had been smothered in it like rancid pig pheromone, before whisked off out a window across roofslates to attics & holes in walls, till traded for Reichsmarks & whisked again, from mamlipapli to the Children's Clinic of the University of Vienna Hospital.

Qwertz snorted as he ran, a headlong stagger, the cripple catching on at last, flappetyflapping at his side, making great strides as a fast learner, survival of the fittest & all that . . . . At an ideal vantage, the eyes in the window tracked the entire brief evolution of the scene below, as the crowd surged & – in a seamlessly choreographed momentum of sheer panic – the two oddities fled up the gravel drive of the Botanical Institute, past the blinking marsupials, pellmell into the unsuspecting shrubbery . . . .

Gep

They came through the trees.
Too many, he couldn't count.
Chasing the man-frog, the hat-&-rag man.
Saw it through the red girl's window,
watching from the books
where no-one could see.
But you could never tell, maybe they had.
Maybe they had & they were coming back.
Back to get him.
Take him to the Other Place.
He ran between the stacks,
down the hall,
down the stairs,
down to the big hole in the ground
where the machines made it safe.
The cats called out to him & he called back.
Mob through the trees, he said.
Man-frog, he said.
Hat-&-rag man.
The cats in the window pricked up their ears.
The machines growled.
The machines went quiet.
They were coming.
He slid down beneath the scaffolds,
by the tilted highchair,
burrowing between the bricks.
Where they wouldn't find him.

Lenoir

Madame Lenoir's reverie was interrupted by the commotion outside in the Jardin, of which the Hexagon commanded a 270-degree view. In preparation for the Household Committee she'd been collating the week's ten-point agenda & the draft minutes from the previous meeting. Yadlun, as if too fatigued by the sight of the construction crew to stand watching at the window any longer, sat slumped at his desk, ogling the patchwork of paperscraps arranged on the blotter – in what, to the uninitiated, could only appear an *impenetrable* system – somewhat, Madame Lenoir might've mused, like a jigsaw puzzle, or a cubist collage. Had she not, of course, known it to be in fact the old man's irreplaceable Grid.

Madame Lenoir crossed the room to see what the commotion was about. There'd been sirens earlier & now there were a dozen or so gendarmes remonstrating with a large crowd as it surged in the direction of the glass pavilions of the Natural History Museum. A great deal of shouting was going on, but the reason for it was far from obvious. She glanced at Yadlun, expecting him to instruct her to make a phone call, but the Director merely stared in silence. In each hand he held a square of ink-smudged paper. His eyes cast a helpless pleading look at the incomplete chessboard pattern on his desk. He seemed, as all too frequently, paralysed by indecision. Perhaps, she thought, he ought to put it all into some sort of computer, so he could just press a button & let it arrange itself. Though probably that wouldn't solve anything, either – he'd still need to be able to bring himself to actually press the button in the first place.

In her reverie, Madame Lenoir had been revisiting the house in Languedoc – pays de Cathares – where, as a grown woman already, she'd nursed her invalid father after her mother died – for how many summers in succession, she'd lost count. Despite a certain superficial resemblance of circumstances, her father had been nothing like Yadlun whatsoever. To begin with, he'd been over seven feet tall, so that even confined to a wheelchair he'd been an imposing wreck. He'd had to stoop most of his life, just to get from one room to another – the sickness had almost been a relief, he'd joked, except for being folded up on himself in the chair like an oversized gimmick.

How, on summer evenings the wind came north-easterly, dispelling the *chaleur*. And the glassy night sky. The heavens in their splendour, their serenity. How she'd sit & watch the pines swaying, the wasps hovering around the lavender, the wilting petunias like mauve & white beach umbrellas, the carpet of rotting cherries, blackberries, figs. The whole engorged food-chain, ants beetles, lizards, flies. And past the walls, a landscape the colour of broken terracotta. Rough, in her mind, as hay stubble, sunflowers, lichen. Her father's wreck, reclining under an arbour, alone with the groaning emptiness of his thoughts. A wicker picnic basket brim-full with pill jars, all that'd remained between this lingering, this dragging-on, & a clean slate.

Hers was a patient discipline of outward appearance & the rigour of a mind capable of supporting it. Had she ever been asked, she might've likened herself to the founders of obscure monastic orders, believing that to possess a soul is more than to stir a bucket of tepid water, disdaining the rippled surface for the murkier sediments, the unconvected depths, the inertial heave of it all in its progress towards stillness.

Afterwards, the emptiness & mortgages drove her away. The disconnected telephone. The actuaries, notaries, lawyers, debt-collectors. Escaping all that. Secretarial school in Toulouse, first, then Paris. Fingernails conscientiously pared. First job typing catalogue cards part-time at the CNRS, rue d'Ulm, on a black L.C. Smith with a vicious carriage-return. Then student records at the Institut du Monde Anglophone on a Minerva portable. Inventory at Gibert&Joseph, alternating between a Corona Coronet Superior & an Electra 110. Then, while temping at the Institute, winter of '68, till they made her & every other union member permanent, upgrading to an Olivetti electric she'd kept ever since. One hundred & eighty per, at its & her best. Behind her now, those days. Somehow having managed to outlast them all. Almost. Almost all.

Schönbrunn

What, Schönbrunn wanted to know, was a tennis umpire's chair doing in the Jardin des Plantes, at the bottom of a great fracking hole? He was standing at the edge of a sheer drop into the maw of an excavation site that filled the courtyard of the Botanical Institute. Or emptied it, rather, he supposed, depending on how you wanted to look at it. Brick-dust caked the toes of his once black oxfords. To make matters worse, it'd begun to drizzle. The red dust made his shoes look like he'd been wading through hardcore crime scenes all morning rather than just tormenting his stomach ulcer at Ma Baker's.

—Well I'll be, Laborde grunted beside him, the smell of curdled flan wafting off his shirt. That's a tennis umpire's chair down the bottom of that great big fracking hole. You reckon it's a clue?

Schönbrunn grated his teeth, suppressing an urge to throw his partner over the edge. It was an irrational urge, no matter how you sized it up. Every known law of physics stood against it: Laborde weighed at least as much as a two-door hatchback, possibly even as much as a small family sedan. He'd've needed a crane, but all the workmen had left behind when they'd been ordered to clear out were a couple of jackhammers, a bobcat, a compressor & a pile-driver – all of which were parked at the bottom of the pit, beside a port-a-loo & the offending piece of furniture. Not much use to anyone down there. A couple of lab boys in white were poking around with grab-sticks & bin-bags.

—It'd take a crane, Laborde yawned.

Schönbrunn felt a sickening in his gut. He gave his partner a sideways glance, but the watery folds of Laborde's own eyes betrayed nothing. Laborde scratched at the crust on his tie & yawned again. Bits of shrivelled flan clung to his fingernails.

—To get all that stuff back out, I mean.

A scaffold descended the far side of the pit with a kind of metal stair zigzagging down it behind strips of nylon mesh. How the workers got in & out. But about the equipment, Laborde was probably right. It pained Schönbrunn only vaguely to admit it: his partner, grotesque as he was, had an uncanny habit of being right about many things. And glancing now back into the pit & at the scaffolding down its far side, this admission gave Schönbrunn further pause.

—Looks like we've got an audience.

Laborde nodded over at one of the windows facing into the courtyard. A half-dozen eyes peered out at them. Schönbrunn squinted into the drizzle. The eyes squinted back. His cop-stare faltered. He blinked but the eyes in the window remained unblinking. Cats. Never a good sign. He levelled his cop-stare at them till his eyes burned & he blinked again, defeated. What was the fracking use?

—Why don't you go interview them, he said morosely. See how your blunt instrument theory holds up.

Laborde grinned. The cats in the window grinned, too. Even the hole in the ground seemed to grin, like it was all a great big fracking joke & he, Schönbrunn, was stuck being the butt of it. Worse, he couldn't even remember what he'd planned to do with his day off, except for sleeping through last night's hangover. Instead he got to spend his time stuck out in the rain with a psychopath covered in baked custard, standing next to a great big hole & being laughed at by a pack of mangy cats, all in the name of upholding law & order. And it was barely afternoon.

—Anything? he shouted down at the lab guys.

One of the white suits looked up, then away again. So much for that. Schönbrunn scanned the courtyard periphery, trying to draw a pattern out of it, the psychic traces of something that in all likelihood didn't exist. The scaffolds swayed. Ghosts fluttered behind the mesh. His mind ached. Even with the dregs of Ma Baker's coffee settling in his intestines, the sleep-deficit was taking its toll. Suddenly all he could think about was nailing his eyes shut & staying that way for the duration.

Coming through the archway behind them, a second forensics team in sanitation gear trod past. With nothing better to do, Schönbrunn observed their progress along the lip of the excavation site, like a troupe of mimes sans bowler hats. It brought back some of the worst imaginable memories of childhood.

—Shite, he muttered, too loud.

—With spangles on, pal, Laborde grunted, fingering his neck-folds. With goddamn spangles on.

In the context, it might've meant anything.

The rain, Schönbrunn couldn't exactly help but notice, was only getting worse. It'd been bound to, like everything else. He was thinking this when his phone rang. Reluctantly he pulled the offending item from his inside coat pocket & eyeballed the screen. His ex-wife's name flashed in pixellated blue.

—All I need, he growled, thumbing the anachronistic little green phone icon.

—DID YOU THREATEN FRANCY, YOU SONOFABITCH?

None of the usual pleasantries – he hadn't even gotten the phone halfway to his ear before she started screaming at him. From the corner of his eye he watched Laborde's grin widen. His ex-wife's voice echoed around the courtyard.

—WHO THE HELL SAID YOU COULD THROW PEOPLE OUT OF MY APARTMENT, YOU FASCIST PRICK?

—C'mon Martine, I'm in the middle of a job, I've got stress.

The forensics guys, having set their gear down by the scaffolds, gawked. The lab boys down in the pit likewise. Even the cats in the window bugged out their eyes. *Jesus*, he thought, *what am I, a free show?*

—I KNOW ALL ABOUT YOUR GODDAMN FRACKING JOB, Schönbrunn's ex screamed even louder. YOU BOTHER ANY OF MY FRIENDS AGAIN, YOU BASTARD, & I'LL HIRE A MOTHERFRACKING CONTRACT KILLER…

Schönbrunn silenced the phone & stuffed it back in his pocket. He'd've liked to murder the smartarse who'd invented that particular species of obnoxious junk, but he'd long ago resigned himself to the odds being stacked against him on that score. The world was full of articles that offended the intelligence of your average self-respecting human of the species, but somehow the idiots in control kept finding room for more. What'd it be next? Driverless fracking cars? Pizza-delivering drones? Robo-cops?

—Women, Schönbrunn muttered, shrugging his slack shoulders to let the audience know the matinee was over.

Laborde yawned. The cats yawned. The forensics guys rummaged through their gear, chuckling. *Ha, ha, fracking ha.* Schönbrunn turned & hunched back out of the courtyard, though the prospect of what awaited in the Jardin was hardly enticement.

Someone else might've discovered all sorts of allegorical significance in the situation at hand, but not Schönbrunn. Staring into a hole in the ground & being chewed-out by his ex-wife in front of an audience was just what it was, nothing more. Life sucked, exactly as they said it did in the classics, but one way or another it was always you who got stiffed with the bill. Was that what'd got Françoise X's head caved in?

He'd tried to form a picture of the crime, but all he came up with was a blur, like watching fastforward reruns of an Olympic sprint. Jesse Owens doing the hundred-yard pseudo rape-o with a steel bar in under ten seconds, more or less, & disappearing into thin air at the end of it. With all the faith in forensics he could muster, the minutes just didn't add up, the actions didn't add up, & the possible motives sure as shit didn't add up.

It was like Miss X'd stepped through a wormhole & come out the other side with a terminal case of DOA. It stank worse than any ectoplasm *he* could imagine. The whole goddamned thing stank. *Sure, pal*, a too familiar voice sounded in his head, *just try pinning this one on aliens & see what that does to brighten your career.*

Schönbrunn came up to the gate & stopped. Laborde, following a few places behind, kicked a pile of gravel with his muddy shoe. The sound of the gravel echoed faintly under the archway & was soon drowned out. On the other side of the gate, it was like the Stade de France on grand-final night.

—What the frack's that all about? Schönbrunn groaned, but even as he did, he knew.

To reach the street they'd've had to run a gauntlet of outraged citizenry & a dozen TV camera crews. Word of the murdered school teacher had obviously spread, just as Schönbrunn had feared, stirring the prurient interest of those segments of society otherwise lacking gainful office-hour employment.

To Schönbrunn's utter disgust, the gendarmerie who were supposed to've been sealing the place off, had allowed a virtual siege to set in. Every degenerate piece of journalistic filth in the country was liable to descend on the scene if someone in authority didn't man-up & put a stop to it. A conclusion which, peering through the bars of the Institute's gate, appeared to Schönbrunn now to be more than foregone.

But even as he watched, & as Laborde watched silently beside him, the situation grew worse still. Much worse.

Godemiché

The only thing audible in the Hexagon was Godemiché pacing back & forth. When he stopped, the silence was complete. He took the occasion to call the meeting to order. Yadlun, meanwhile, was staring out the window as per his recent habit & said nothing. The young researcher, Gachette, was sitting listlessly across the conference table with her arms crossed & a laptop balanced skewiff on her knee.

Madame Lenoir, poised with her stenographer's pad, couldn't help but notice that Godemiché had positioned himself at such an angle as to see inside the top of Gachette's blouse. Gep, however, was nowhere to be seen – not lingering behind the bookshelves, as he usually would – perhaps he'd caught the telltale change of light against the parquet, from the sudden stillness of the machines in the courtyard. After the pilings had been set with concrete, the pile-driver had ceded its place to some other sort of machine with a high arc. Its complicated shadow had roamed around the Institute for a short while then come to a stop.

Godemiché had just begun to elaborate the new scheduling procedure he'd designed to replace The Grid, announcing a subcommittee for its implementation & oversight. He proposed himself, the jejune presumptive, to chair the committee. Madame Lenoir sighed. So this was what it'd come to finally, the fatal succession: Godemiché dividing up & apportioning to himself Yadlun's household in the old man's very presence. Ransacking his thanedom, Consigning his Domesday Books to oblivion.

Godemiché's audience stared blankly at nothing. Such, Madame Lenoir pondered, does History make bystanders of us all. Yadlun himself appeared oblivious. She might've felt pity, but something in the man's hypnotic attitude proffered a kind of sanctuary from itself. Almost a beatitude. His stark transformation – gilded by this epidemic of tedium into which Godemiché had plunged them – caused her mind to drift back to the moment from which her own chosen path, uncomplicated by hope, desire or faintest ambition, had diverged from what in contrast might yet be called life.

Madame Lenoir had no regrets, the impulse was merely what it was, an impulse, a diffusion of electrostatic in the brain. Had she ever born a child, she'd've wished it to be Yadlun, unconditionally. She'd've followed him into extinction, if he'd shown any such initiative. One could only admire his stoic ambivalence. Greater things spoke to him. He was a man who sat all night on an umpire's chair, watching the stars among stray cats. The ancients would've called him holy. Perhaps he was simply mad.

At that moment Godemiché stammered & Madame Lenoir was forced to look up. The Presumptive's renewed pacing had taken him across the room & now he was standing beside Yadlun, staring out the window. Yadlun was faintly smiling. Sensing something, Gachette stood up. There were police in the courtyard, she exclaimed. A faint current of excitement ran through the Institute. Finally, a real drama. Godemiché waved his agenda lamely. History was evading him & he knew it. And then a knock came at the door.

Mahnood

Sub-Commandante Lacepède Vargas glanced back in horror at the swarm of marsh monsters crashing after them through the mangroves. Something must've happened to the time co-ordinates, plunging him back into some mid-evolutionary event. Unless, of course, the engineers on Poincaré VI had got it completely arseways & this wasn't the past at all, *but the future*. *Planet of the Apes* stuff. But all *that* was academic at this point. The only thing that mattered now was getting to some open water, where he could put his flippers to good use. Coz even with this half-humanoid's helping hand, he was still a sitting duck. In a manner of speaking. A fish out of water. A salamander in a rat race.

Qwertz

Denying the ideal & everything that follows from it, as once said that rancid pornographer Courbet, *I fully approach the emancipation of democracy* . . . . Boohoo . . . . But if they thought he, Qwertz-of-the-People, was about to stand still for a lynching, they had another thing coming . . . . *Vive la foutre!* . . . . He could hear the litany of just desserts pursuing them from afar . . . . A revolution, after all, knew nothing better than to parody itself . . . . Like a mob in hot pursuit of a pair of sad sacks . . . . By cunning manoeuvres they'd kept one schlep ahead of their fate . . . . What next? The cripple made a high keening sound . . . . Wordlessly his expressions pleaded . . . . To be saved, to be left to die, Qwertz couldn't tell . . . .

He urged the dysplasiac on . . . . Humid plantlife concealed their progress through the glasshouse . . . . Past the display of ichthofossils, the shrill panes singing in the light of their reflections . . . . Face to face with extinction they stoically breathed, gained bearings, took the measure of their pursuers, consulted the oracle of their fear . . . . Clairvoyance had never been Qwertz's forte, but it was a good bet they ought to keep moving before someone wised up . . . . Past the Victoria Regia, the Titan Arum, the Zaminkand, the Elephant Foot . . . . It would've made a splendid setting for an orgy of chained man-eating cunts . . . . *Nine Brides in a Deadman's Bed* . . . . He made a mental note of it: flesh-pink, sanguine, miroir verte, iridescent nacre.

But having found their way into the glasshouse, Qwertz was at a loss as to how to get back out . . . . To reach the far side, a back-gate through the Jardin's encircling wall, the street & freedom . . . . He pulled his flippered accomplice to a halt, cast worrisome glances hither & yon among the unsympathetic foliage . . . . Plants are less egotistical than they are partial, he'd once been assured, by an expert in the field . . . . A companionable neighbour of the Widow Fondane, fond of the young Klotz . . . . Taught him to yank-off behind the balcony ficcus dribbling snail slime on the dying leaves . . . . The shock of recognition the first time the old pederast's hand travelled down the front of his shorts . . . . A Raft-of-the-Medusa look of desperation had come as naturally to him then as now . . . . Had he been permitted to witness it, an entire series of mediocre tableaux might immediately've suggested themselves, in a flash of erstwhile inspiration, delayed action, or sheer derangement . . . . Anything to escape the dawning cognisance – elaborated to the very end of its necessary implications – that he, Qwertz, & this veritable liability he'd so witlessly affixed himself to, were now quite righteously & proverbial fucked . . . .

He glanced at the dysplasiac whose own eyes wandered hypnotically in autonomous orbits like an idiot in the throes of religious ecstasy . . . . God only knew by what telepathy the unleggèd creature grasped their predicament . . . .

Oh humanity!

Just then a raucous shout came from the other side of the *fogged* panes . . . . *They're onto us for sure this time!* The enlarging shape of something suspiciously like a projectile . . . . Qwertz initiated an unsteady plunge between the man-eating ferns, carnivorous vines, rapacious flowers oozing with carnal stench – Manhood in tow . . . . There was, as they say in such situations, a loud crashing sound . . . . Glass rained . . . . Strewed with plant-matter, the fugitives tumbled through the shadows . . . . Down some steps . . . . Into a low vaulted tunnel . . . . Flutters of war-weary dèja-vu . . . .

Hosanna! Qwertz genuflected, face plastered to the floor, *We're saved!*

Red brick oozed a mineral slime . . . . To all appearances an ancient conduit, sultry to an appalling degree . . . . Fossilised footsteps tracking luminous into the netherworld – *mortichnia* – dissolving a dozen metres hence into a sluice . . . . Flappetyflap the dysplasiac leapt into the water & – casting those uncanny eyes pleadingly back – swam forth with unnerving fluency . . . . Qwertz, less afraid to drown than of the alternatives, flung himself in recklessly after, mind conjuring tropical rats, carnivorous flukes, man-eating mosquitoes . . . . Soon he was a sodden weight of herringbone clogging the works . . . . *Wait!* he shrieked, feeling the rope already round his neck . . . . Elbows & knees gouging the brickwork with septuagenarian ferocity . . . .

Schönbrunn

In the space of an hour the mob had doubled in size around the palatial glasshouse where dead Miss Françoise X had been showing her eight-year old school kids the fossil of an extinct fish some time that morning, before parties unknown put an iron bar through her skull & smothered her in ectoplasm. It was, the sign just visible over the heads in the crowd said, the MUSÉUM NATIONAL D'HISTOIRE NATURELLE. Schönbrunn doubted it was regularly this popular.

An unconvincing phalanx of six or seven uniformed gendarmes were all that stood between the mob & the glassed-in tropical plants. A dozen or more panes had already succumbed under a heavy barrage of paving stones, which for the time being at least seemed to've come to a halt. Whether due to timely police intervention or an exhaustion of the available supply of missiles, it was impossible to tell. Abused greenery rustled in the unfamiliar breeze.

Schönbrunn & Laborde came down the path, projecting intent. Schönbrunn with his right hand flexing, Laborde prying his holster away from the sweaty folds of polyester gathered in a knot under his left oxter. Once at the frontline, Schöbrunn worked his cop-stare at the agitators nearest at hand. He recognised a couple of faces: the truculent headmaster, the kiosk attendant, one of the gardeners. There were even a couple of school kids wielding sharpened sticks.

—Shite, muttered the detective.

A gendarme edged up beside him, a nervous look on his face.

—Sir?

—Cut the *sir* crap & tell me what the hell's going on here.

—They reckon the ones who did it are inside, sir.

—Did what?

—The dead school teacher, sir.

—*What?*

—Some Arab & a vagrant. Apparently identified at the scene, sir. According to the, er, witnesses, they took refuge in the big glasshouse, sir.

Schönbrunn grabbed the gendarme's shirtfront.

—And why the frack wasn't I told this before?

—Dunno, sir, it happened so quick. They said they were gonna go in there & lynch 'em. Reckon if we don't get out of the way, they'll lynch us too.

—Jesus Christ! Can't you people do a goddamn thing right? This whole fracking place should've been locked-down HOURS AGO. Who's giving the orders round here?

—Aren't you, sir?

Laborde grinned.

—Can't win, pal.

Schönnnbrunn shook his head & let the fistful of shirt go.

—Nah, he snarled, I'm just the shithead they dragged in from his day off.

He turned in disgust to face the crowd.

—Ain't no-one doing any lynching round here, he said.

He stepped forward, hands folded over his belt buckle.

—YOU GOT THAT? he shouted. NO LYNCHING ON MY SHIFT! Now go home before I book the lot of you.

The mob was still, no-one said a word. Schönbrunn turned to Laborde,

—Guess we ought to go inside & see what all this's about. Get a statement or something.

Laborde took out a handkerchief & mopped the sweat from his chin. Grunted. Schönbrun turned back & eyed the crowd. None of them had moved, they were watching him intently, like a herd of cattle. It spooked him. He eyed his partner.

—You really think there's something to that ecto-crap?

—Got any better ideas? Laborde drawled.

—Yeah, maybe they've got some sort of alien plant in one of them glass boxes inside there.

He jerked his head in the direction of the glasshouse.

—Triffid stuff. Been experimenting on it with radiation or something. Genetic modification crap. Got loose. Fancied itself some extra protein. Cottoned onto Miss Bow-Peep. Clobbered her with a steel bar to put us off the scent.

—Pal, Laborde grinned, if they ever pin a medal on someone for this job, I hope it's you. You're the only cop I know who truly deserves it.

—Shite, Schönbrunn dead-panned. With spangles on.

Then a voice rose from the edge of the crowd. Schönbrunn caught sight of a fat middle-aged woman in a floral housecoat. She was pointing away from the glasshouse, towards the rear of the Institute. The gate, through which Schönbrunn & Laborde had only minutes before exited, stood negligently ajar. What now? Did the old bat think she was their mother?

—THERE! the woman yelled. They're in THERE!

The mob came alive. Before Schönbrunn had time to react, dozens of vigilantes had surged up the gravel drive & were shoving through the gate. The hinges gave way in moments & the whole thing crashed to the ground. The mob stampeded through the arch. The woman's voice rose to a scream.

—HANG 'EM HIGH!

Schönbrunn had a moment's panic, about the forensics guys in their white suits, unarmed, oblivious to what was about to befall them.

Then, from the courtyard, came an almighty crash.

Holoptychius

It was a dead cert, fishboy's days were numbered. If something stank, it was probably him. A suspect entity. A fossilitic ex-junkie turd. At the end of his proverbial rope, he'd taken his last dive, wrapped in that old green&purple cape, plastic vampire fangs, glistening baldpatch framed by greasy cords of matted fish-hair, stones tied (not very convincingly) to emaciated fins, right down into the Seine. Just another wannabe rock'n'roll suicide no-one ever heard of. Well no-one had ever thought to teach a fish to swim, either, so Holopychius just sank like a stone, straight through the floor of the abyss, down into the substrate, the sewers & catacombs & secret chambers of the city's burst & buried ventricle, the dead heart, the whatever. Fishboy came-to splattering on a slab of funereal marble, in a place of dank humid confinement. Somehow he'd washed up on almost dry land. He wasn't sure if this was good luck or something worse. He tuned his fish-ears for the sound of rats. There was a faint buzzing, as of insect life among tropical ferns. Or a dead TV. Or brain static. He dug his trusty zippo out to take a looksee. A face loomed straight out of the blackness at him. Holoptychius was fit to crap himself to death, but on account of many years of narcotic abuse the old intestines disobliged. Pale, beaknosed, with a piece of seaweed slung across its forehead. Fishboy stared. The face stared back. Fishboy blinked. The face didn't. That was all there was to it. After a while, the zippo sputtered out. Flap-flap-flap. Invisible wings, mists, auguries. Finally he woke another flame out of the lighter. The face, of course, was still there, attached to a marble head with a marble wig, attached to a marble bust, with marble writing on it, difficult under the circumstances to unriddle from the diligent mildews. Some vague columnar forms discernible in the gloom. A place redolent, so to speak, of expired mythologies. Or a communal bathroom in some formerly upmarket establishment that, like him, had seen comparatively better days. The plumbing amounted to an open conduit, spilling across undulant carpets of slime. Water gushed & sucked, gurgled & puked. Thus from untimely suicide had he, Holoptychius Fishboy, been borne. Hence. Of egress, signs there were none. In such circumstances, feelings of forlornness would not be untypical. Fishboy slumped back against the cold slab. "Looks like it's just me & you, pal," he told the character with the wig. From the pocket of his Levis he dug a battered harmonica & commenced to draw atrocious sounds from it, puffing his lips out, sucking them in. *Well gee I wish I were dead, ma, if it's all the same to you. But I think I'll be stuck here a long while more, adrift on this river of poo…* Which was the exact moment the creatures sprang upon him. Well, not upon, exactly. But coughing & flapping, heaving up out of the drain, half-man half-frog half-stick insect, utterly sodden. They lay there in a heap, gaping in a type of factional wonderment. The zippo's flame wavered, but that was all. "My god," the stick one finally managed, ogling him unashamedly, "it's a fish!"

Yadlun

Godemiché stood in the middle of the Hexagon, triumphant, arm &
outstretched finger pointing at the cowed figure of Yadlun, a shadow
of his former shadow, framed against the open window from which,
moments before, he'd witnessed the Institute's invasion, like a diseased
paspalum.

—Aid & succour to the enemy! Godemiché shrieked.

Madame Lenoir stared brainshocked from her stenographer's
desk. Gachette was nowhere to be seen, having fled among the stacks
at the first sounds of incursion. A mob, decked-out in trophies seized
from the hapless forensic's crew, had very suddenly appeared at the
top of the stairs & were now spilling into the Hexagon. It seemed as if
no sooner had the commotion begun in the courtyard than the entire
Institute was overwhelmed.

—It's him, Godemiché shrieked again. He's the one you want!

The mob, undecided, eyed Yadlun while Godemiché, seizing his
golden opportunity, shrieked even louder:

—KILL THE TRAITOR!

Someone lobbed a chunk of brick – it sailed across the room &
caught Godemiché square on the side of the head. The Assistant
Director groaned sickly & went slack at the knees. The mob took their
cue & surged. Madame Lenoir, caught in their path, perceived her
martyrdom.

—Vive Montségur! she gasped, as one who talks in their sleep.

But before the mob could reach him, Yadlun, with the unexpected
agility of a cat, & defying every appearance of helplessness, vaulted the
windowsill to liberty.

Gachette

An eerie quietness had fallen upon the Institute. The flood, so to speak, had ebbed, the chaos receded, the tumult detumesced. Peering between bookshelves, Gachette perceived only darkness interspersed with shafts of dusking light. A receding echo of footsteps outside on the gravel, shouts far distant, the faintest crackling sound as of leaves stirred by a breeze. Only there was no breeze. The musty air tasted ashen, like an aftertaste of fear.

Gachette could barely swallow, would not have been able to form words had she wanted to. Instead she crouched behind the shelves, waited, listened, watched. The crackling grew. The air became darker. A sudden fatigue weighed heavily upon her. She might've drifted into sleep had her mind not registered the scene evolving beyond the Hexagon's threshold.

It had all the appearance of discoloured celluloid projected on a screen, with a figure dancing on it. A figure with arms like a tree. Glowing branches with leaves of flame. It called to mind icons in stained glass windows, objects of strange veneration. Gachette blinked, coughed, groped for support. Her mind reeled. The Tree Man of Borneo, the Sacred Heart, the Burning Bush. The figure twisted, flailed, fell & rose, grew sizably till it filled the doorway. And then it howled.

The moment it did so, Gachette knew it for what it was. Madame Lenoir, ablaze, staggered out into the vestibule & collapsed onto the floor. The carpet blackened as if a hole had opened around the dying woman to swallow her up. Fire spread out from the doorjambs, licking at the ceiling, the walls, the book shelves. Smoke billowed. Gachette knelt there utterly transfixed, like a child before a video screen. Her eyes watered, her lungs ached.

Gep

The courtyard echoed with the din
of surrounding chaos,
like a theatre
staging an argument with itself.
Flames licked faintly at the windows.
The cats mewled.
Gep,
burrowing out from under the rubble.
Yadlun,
folded in half
across the twisted umpire's chair.
The siege had lifted,
had spread to running battles through the Jardin.
Gep
gazed upward
at the window from which Yadlun had leapt.
A square of orange light flickered.
The conflagration spread
quickly through the upper floors.
Glass shattered.
Above the roofline,
against the smoked-blacked sky,
a plastic shopping bag,
caught in a tree,
shimmered like a blood moon.
Faintly Gep keened,
cradled the deadman's head.
The cats,
congregating all around,
keened also.

Part II

Françoise X

A true account of my death [   ] would begin with a perforated line,
[   ] separating a darkness you can see [   ] from a darkness you can't.
[   ] The perforations are as innocent [   ] as a trail of ants. [   ] In
my dream [   ] which isn't a dream, [   ] I'm as small as an ant. [   ]
It begins with some immeasurably large presence, [   ] something
hunched in the sky, [   ] though it isn't really the sky, [   ] like an
articulated mountain [   ] or a giant pair of hands, [   ] folding the
night-world along that perforated line [   ] & beginning to tear. [   ]
The tear runs as far as I can see [   ] & as far as I can't. [   ] And
when the darkness comes apart, [   ] I come apart with it. [   ] Inside,
[   ] I'm full of tiny luminous ants. [   ] It's then my murderers sneak
towards me, [   ] out of the torn world. [   ] I can't see them, [   ]
but I know they're there. [   ] I have no clue to their identity: [   ]
I *am* that clue. [   ] They're shapelessness [   ] wanders in & out of
focus. [   ] A stain on the eye. [   ] A stain in the stain of the eye.
[   ] As they close in, [   ] it's impossible to know [   ] even where
to look. [   ] Also, [   ] by the time they reach me, [   ] I'm not there
anymore. [   ] The ants carry me [   ] into remote corners. [   ] As I
come apart [   ] I'm born in reverse, [   ] like a Jewish-Quarter clock.
[   ] The backwards hands turn. [   ] They tear & they turn. [   ]
Divided among the multitude, [   ] I'm burrowed inwards. [   ] The
ants murmur me. [   ] Time has many dimensions. [   ] My body is
no longer [   ] a contained substance, [   ] but there's language here.
[   ] Words are rushing [   ] at the speed of light [   ] yet thought
stands still. [   ] A trillion neurons [   ] in a fixed firmament. [   ]
Perhaps I've passed [   ] to the other side [   ] of the impossible. [   ]
Perhaps the impossible [   ] has traversed me. [   ]

The Ants

The witness accounts begin & end as we do. An underground radius of electricity.

Nights deliquesce, boiled in formic acid. "Abandoned" comes before "abased." In the ensuing, her front tooth severed a nerve, lapsed sideways. Breathing a neutrino atmosphere, as in a salt mine. Vaginal clench.

By subdivision, diazepam, reader of panegyrics.

They have extraction down to a fine art. In the treatment of bipolar disorder, depression, schizophrenia: atypically. A child in a tree. Certain forms of neglected or repressed association.

Now, for example.

They've forgotten the secret of knowing the question before it does. To empiricise from hoarded rubbish, human sediment.

Fragments, of all things ultimately. Word-nests.

The moon mid-orbit on its struts, its slates. Brainstem, sliced in DNA alcohol. Each cell like a peninsula combines in opposition. Twenty-eight years. Her Saturn-return.

The insect quorum, the gynaecological chair: coal-ballasted. On this benighted foreboding light was shed.

Levels of intensity arisen from detonation.

Egress. In the east rose the pyrocumulus. Permission adduced by fait accompli, to re-name. They prayed, foreheads to the sand. Bone of sperm whale. The oneiric genome.

Agreement. Aggrievement.

Like us, consciousness brings death into being.

Insert diagram: preparation before the eating of flesh. A telephone booth. The number you don't know how to dial. There were men without facial insignia, carrion crow-people beating the waves in awakening syncopation. Waves in recurrent megatonnage.

You dreamt them, they were real.

Followed by a gap. Its habitat was now an ocean floor by omission. There're greater aversions than phenomenology. The monstrous races of men & beasts were sublimates of fear. Stumbling before first encountering solidity. Until that point, hypochondria, to fold-over, to lick. A theory is the summation of a fact only after.

In the name of God, she said.

They sealed the unidentified body in a lead box to forestall transmission, nacre. Amphetamine had long ceased to have appreciable effects. Telepathy without abating over time or longeur. In the poetic-functionalist terrain, taxation applies only to increase. Quicksilver turning black from inside. Their reports caused only distress. In case of emergency, assume the following position.

In her eyes like alters of sacrifice, their oriflammes.

Some spoke of apparitions with flat heads. Before consuming, the top of the skull had been removed.

First the jaw, later in the gut. After source-code reanimation, to meet light halfway. Prior to warning, immersion's totality. A verbal depth-sounding. Traction to nerve squall: centrifuged. To break into sections, reason demands outflux. Destitute in its autonomous moment.

The parentheses open but don't resemble again.

Diversionary forensics: each search area is divided by an integer to volte-face. The ratio of conductivity of the erogenous zones. At that moment two blackholes colliding, the socalled knot of life. As of a victim.

At root, the neuropathologene, forced, excavating.

You learn to breathe by attempting to drown. Other factors at play. Irreversibility, for example.

The Mob

Get 'em!

    Pute de con de merde d'Arabe!

Catch 'em!

    Pute de con de merde de Juif!

Grab 'em!

    Morte aux Arabes!

Hold 'em!

    Morte aux Juifs!

Strip 'em!

    Sales Arabes!

Tie 'em!

    Sales Juifs!

Beat 'em!

    Sale fils de pute!

Bang 'em!

    Mahomet est un cochon!

Bash 'em!

    La France aux Français!

Bruise 'em!

    Arabes dehors!

Scar 'em!

    Juifs dehors!

Tear 'em!

    Vive la France!

Tar 'em!

    Vive le Front National!

Skin 'em!

    À bas les kebabs!

Break 'em!

    À bas les bagels!

Gouge 'em!

    Pas de halal!

Hang 'em!

    Pas de kosher!

Stone 'em!

Brain 'em!

Shoot 'em!

Boil 'em!

Drown 'em!

Chop 'em!

Slice 'em!

Spit on 'em!

Piss on 'em!

Shit on 'em!

Torture 'em!

Lacerate 'em!

Mutilate 'em!

Flay 'em!

Bugger 'em!

Blind 'em!

Castrate 'em!

Strangle 'em!

Behead 'em!

Meurtriers du Christ!

Réfuseurs du porc!

Dehors les musulmans!

Dehors les infidels!

Salauds d'Arabes!

Salauds de Juifs!

Salauds de noirs!

Salaud flics!

Salauds de salauds!

Morte aux sauvages!

Morte aux circoncisés!

Putes à nègres!

Putes à bougnoules!

À bas les gros nez!

À bas les sodomites!

Voleurs de poules!

Vendeurs de porno!

France aux patriotes!

France aux culs!

Crush 'em!

Morte aux collabos!

Smite 'em!

Étrangers dehors!

Dismember 'em!

Morte aux profiteurs!

Obliterate 'em!

Sauf les blancs!

Burn 'em!

Nom de Dieu!

Bury 'em!

Mangeurs d'agneau!

Pulverise 'em!

Terroristes!

Electrocute 'em!

Violeurs!

Eat 'em!

Cannibales!

Etcetera!

Etcetera!

Myrmecophobia

A siege has nothing to do with the molecular physics of a swarm rushing over your body. You may be under siege right now, without knowing it. How *will* you know it? How will you recognise it if, & when, it occurs? If it's already occuring?

Perhaps this's only the first phase. The subterfuge. The incursion by stealth. The subtle positioning before the true siege begins? To allow you time to think about it. To feed your paranoias. Nuance your hypochondrias. Encourage you to rush around absurdly repairing your defences. Hatching unworkable contingency plans. Concocting an unfounded optimism. Exhausting yourself in the enumeration of every possible uncertainty, on the pretext of thereby gaining the upper hand.

The truth is, you're no less in the dark than you were to begin with.

What will come next? How will you resist? Will you resist? What will be the consequences? Will you survive? Will they let you survive? Will you know if you've survived?

Already the siege-to-come is creating a prison for you. A body for your incarceration. You've felt it. In your mind it's there, an automaton immaculate in polished mica. But the closer you examine it, searching for flaws, for a crack in the edifice, for a means of defeating it, of escaping it, the more complicated, the more *compelling* this insect-hive becomes.

Like an infinite mirror maze.

A brain fungus.

Inflationary economics.

Dark matter swallowing the cosmos.

The Umpire's Chair

A world view
to an ant

is as a utopia
to an empiricist.

The Rhyming Tree

Around me wind
        the winds that chime
the newborn crime,
        the ancient rime –
to never mourn
        the never-seen,
to ill-conceive
        the never-been.
From the bones
        of Time I shrive
the roots of life,
        of dream, of strife.
My secret commune
        knows no end,
I do not bow
        to god or man –
but cast my shade
        on kings & priests,
& children, beggars,
        burghers, thieves,
& bare my boughs
        to lovers' necks,
to hoist them, heave
        them, break them hence.
For the Rhyming
        Tree am I,
conjoining all
        who live & die,
the sun & rain
        & earth & sky,
the days to come
        & those gone by.

The Scaffold

Swing low, sweet Charity…

The Hole

its desires were fathomless once brought to light. dug-up trepanned
archaeologised. secrets left to chance. occult wells of air. a will-always-
done. points without contradiction. hieratic moons. a cross on sharpened
stone. dawn birdsong. ancient plastic. grenade pin. faith of a hundred.
a dog's hip bone. bottle cap. cyclotron. toll bridge. a ten-way switch. a
fountainhead. another matter. whose valley home. gaseous letters. a gay
rosette. the search for facts. Marshall Plan dollars. a subcritical mass.
literature & creative urges. immoral pragmatisms. Bhagavad-Gita.
pilgrim fathers. scattered worlds. the nape of Louis XVI's neck. the
radiance of a thousand suns. black forces. images of flight bedded in
clay. a thousand promises. flesh-mottled texture. a vision of fate. warn,
rough, rising from the narrow spar. El Greco. mouldy scraps parcels
crumbs. a one-clock bomb. pages & dimensions. guilty routines. asemic
interference. two bits. colloidal graphite. waterlogged. an embalmed
carrier pigeon. wax record. hotel letterhead. stubbornness. the wind
that blows down dead & hollow trees. a subterranean spring. sacrificial
rites. the Manhattan Project. staccato. a worm that turned. picture
frames. sewer-holes. burning glass. a touch in the dark. Patagonia. an
all-significant core. its own sake. a box camera. the demonic power. a
crucifixion. engineering materials. radium. a clown-like suit. China.
the return-waves of an echo. Eau de Vichy. in a coldly distracted &
mechanical fashion. social welfare. Algiers. rheumatoid arthritis. x-ray.
hysteresis. war surplus. rhythmic suggestion. opera glasses. democratic
fantasies. the purpose of reproduction. Piltdown Man's other jawbone.
dirty laundry. simultaneous translations. a stone garden. notched beams.
black-scorched birds. a cloud. a skull. the general tone of the meaning.
litmus paper. silence. the guts of the last priest. a stance. lordship. a
new social bond. from pale to blue to grey. bone ash. egolessness. veins
of ant traffic. brick escarpment. pourings. cycle-time. bleeding hands.
bitumen. days required. ditching of all types. cosmic heat. overburden.
the urge to please. muckpiles. riprap. dolomite. yellow flowers. fine
aggregate. a throne. an epilepsy. jaw plates. switchboards. burden
standards. things not said. failure. composted plastic. Vercingetorix.
night-time theatres. headaches neuralgia vomiting. the first fruit. a
solace. bore-water. signs of doom. stress relief. PC monitors. REM

sleep. *sui generis* meanderings. sailors lighting flares. fossilised shock waves. occipito-temporo-parietal. a butterfly machine. a worm machine. the length of an index finger. spilt milk. blast designs. the internet of things. hunters burrowers weavers. silicate. slitted cats' eyes. arrest warrants. watch lists. lettres cachets. topographical wallpaper. broken windows. the spirit of '68 of '44 of '71 of '48 of '32 of '89. the *Protocols of Paris*. six million willing collaborationists. interspecific violence. the steam off a Roman's piss. your avid look.

The Disinterrogation Routine

Nothing inside a hole, they said.
Nothing?
But having said everything once, there was no need to repeat it.
Even in variation.

The Forces of Public Order

Dusk comes on.

Flaming torches drift through the teargas.

Loud hailers & incomprehensible ultimatums.

The invisible mob.

Riot cops ranked at the Jardin gates.

Nervous.

Stamping.

Rumour of pagan sacrifice.

Supernatural occurrences.

Aliens.

Fear whispers its way among the raw recruits sweating in their riot armour.

Fear sweating through their eyes.

The Cats

Where be your gibes now?

The Fugitives

If it be the names of seaports that give shape to the sea, it is the secret that gives shape to what some call the Underworld & others, with an ear attuned to the portentous, call the Great Despond. For there are those who deem the Below a place of despair & those, despairing of its redemption to the light, who deem it Unknowable. In their minds it is a dark shapeless morass, whose epithets alone give shape to its shapelessness.

History is full of last spectres drifting off, alone or in company, hunched into a prevailing wind. A tunnel, perhaps. A road bearing dead into the setting sun. Into the moon. Into the pitch blackness. The gate, the mouth, the maw of "hell" cropped out with sinister shadows, etc. "Barrière d'Enfer." Like some ancient lugubrious Métro entrance with ticketbooth & turnstile. *Denfert-Rochereau.* Where amateur cataphiles descend into the headless King's tombe-issoires, along once submerged coastlines & lagoon sediments, medieval rhizomic quarries of Lutetian limestone, gypsum, plaster of Paris turned to bone repositories. In the vague belief, not wholly unfounded, that the hidden meaning of the City lies in the patient ruminations of its substrate.

The quest for knowledge, no less.

The *signatura rerum* constellated in the Cosmic Tree.

For such a purpose have many species of fool scoured the sepulchral passageways of the Underworld. But not only. And not always fools.

Yet if this be the proverbial Cave of the ancient philosophs, the realm of the benighted, of the simulacral, of unreal dream & too-real nightmare, wherefore is the light? Those, contented to be mere heliotropes, may stare at the sun. Others seek a more inner-light. Others still seek the Absolute, the light that is nothing: darkness radiant. And those, instruments of chance, Reason's subproletariat, who seek nothing but to subsist, to escape one moment for the next, who flee the past to be entrapped by the future, who know nothing more than to breathe, to eat & not be eaten. For now. For the next five minutes. (Oh, but they know who *you* are.) Thus are eternities spun into a web whose anchors are forever drifting in the mobile gloom of the *sous sol.* Among the sluices & canals, the weirs, the conjoining tunnels, buttresses, dead-ends, broken shafts, the ratholes, pneumatic tubes, wormlairs & conduits, the labyrinthine motherboards of chemically-castrated Turing machines, secret influencing machines, adding machines, analytic machines, Panopticon machines, push-button flush machines, self-inventory Cosmo-Demonological machines…

If you dug far enough, through all those convoluted convolutions, y'd reach the Han Dynasty.

So they say.

The truth is, these are the entrails of Power. And through them flows an excrement loaded with blood-guilt most palpable.

It is the conscience of the world few cast their gaze upon. They come only to view the prettified bones of the nameless. A morbid little sideshow alley, of regimented skulls & femurs & funerary monuments. The disinterred *intra mural* dead, carted hence in their six millions at the behest of Property. The dead as commodification's landfill, recycled into the void produce by the inexorable rise of Capital as if out of the very "bowels of the Earth."

An edifying spectacle. (No end to its labours, even for the perished. It is the hand-that-never-lets-go. There *are no fugitives*.)

The Lynching

1. At what point did their attempted escape through the sewer deliver the fugitives directly into the hands of the mob?

2. By what itinerary did they reach their final destination?

3. Was the setting sun magnified in the glasshouse?

4. Did the fugitives mistake their captors for saviours? Or did they stumble blindly to their fate?

5. By what magnitude was the dim light at the end of the tunnel as a ray of undiluted truth to the flagrant obscurities cast by a zippo lighter?

6. When precisely did day turn into night?

7. Did they protest their innocence?

8. Were they judged impartially, in accordance with the evidence acquired & the statutes handed down, upon the authority of the people & the revolutionary council?

9. Was the principle of habeas corpus applied?

10. What verdict was pronounced?

11. Who pronounced it?

12. Did the fugitives fit their own description?

13. Were they guilty by virtue of being seized, or by virtue of being defenceless?

14. Which of the two was the first to be strung up?

15. Was the tree chosen at random or for some higher significance?

16. Were the authorities complicit or were they powerless to intervene?

17. Did the punishment fit the crime?

18. Was the smoothness of the rope with which they were hanged like the smoothness of modern architecture, of polished steel, of power?

19. Where was the true culprit in all of this?

20. And what about the fish? Was the fish supernumerary to the scales of Justice? Or was it literally the one that got away? Or did the mob run out of rope? Or was the fish merely a bookish conceit, an archaic semaphore, a proxy for vague credulities? Existing to show the way by the light of allegory? That, whichever path He may take, Man cannot escape His martyrdom, amen? Does it matter whether or not we believe in it (the fish, fate, justice, literature)? Is this the end?

The Plot

Whereof one cannot speak.

or:

Lost. Lost. All lost.

Part III

Schönbrunn

The two detectives gazed morosely at the scene. Between them, boredom met indifference in unequal combat. Exhaustion, bitterness. Schönbrunn couldn't remember anymore when it'd begun. Labord merely shrugged his shoulder pads, turned the colour of week-old urine in the morbid halflight.

—It ain't over yet, Schönbrunn snarled, watching the emergency crew cut the two hanged men down from the baobab tree.

The mob had melted away with the teargas as finally the morning sun broke through. Schönbrunn blinked at it angrily – it looked like it was going to be a fine day. In the distance a loudhailer crackled. Sirens converged. Somebody had hooked a cardboard sign around one of the hanged men's necks. It'd fallen onto the ground. Schönbrunn couldn't be bothered going over to see what was written on it. Who cared what idiots had to say for themselves? He sure as hell didn't. Laborde stepped past the bodybags & picked it up, turned it over, tossed it aside. Shrugged once more. In an almost choreographed synchronicity they both tilted their heads & peered up at the dangling ropes simultaneously.

A little way off in the shadows, eyes glinting in the light, Gep crouched, observing the two cops. They looked funny staring up at the tree. Like the old broken cat-man in the chair watching the sky.

While they stared at the tree, the ambulance men carried the hat&rag man & the man-frog away in sacks.

Then after a while the fat cop stood back over beside the angry cop.

—Shite, the angry one spat.

The fat one picked his nose with his little finger & inspected the snot wedged under the dirty crescent of nail.

—It's like they say in the movies, pal, the fat cop drawled, ain't never over. And was about to add, as an afterthought, *Till it starts again.* But didn't.

[NO END]